I Will Fear No Evil

Other Books by Debbie Viguié

The Psalm 23 Mysteries

The Lord is My Shepherd
I Shall Not Want
Lie Down in Green Pastures
Beside Still Waters
Restoreth My Soul
In the Paths of Righteousness
For His Name's Sake
Walk Through the Valley
The Shadow of Death

The Kiss Trilogy

Kiss of Night
Kiss of Death
Kiss of Revenge

Sweet Seasons

The Summer of Cotton Candy
The Fall of Candy Corn
The Winter of Candy Canes
The Spring of Candy Apples

Witch Hunt

The Thirteenth Sacrifice
The Last Grave
Circle of Blood

I Will Fear No Evil

Psalm 23 Mysteries

By Debbie Viguié

Published by Big Pink Bow

I Will Fear No Evil

Copyright © 2014 by Debbie Viguié

ISBN-13: 978-0-9906971-1-4

Published by Big Pink Bow

www.bigpinkbow.com

Dedicated to my darling Schrödinger, and all the other black cats out there in need of loving homes. I pray they find them.

Thank you to Laurie Aguayo for her costume suggestion for Mark and Traci (Dick Tracy and Breathless Mahoney). Thank you to Kristi Hirtzel for her costume suggestion for Mark and Traci (Dick Tracy and Tess Trueheart). Thank you to Chrissy Current for her costume suggestion for Geanie and Joseph (Morticia and Gomez Addams). Thank you to Serena Webb, Pam Weger, Katie Armistead, and Kylie Marie Bates for their suggestion of a Zorro costume for Jeremiah. Thank you also to my husband, Scott, my parents Rick and Barbara, and my dear friend Calliope for all their love and support.

1

Rabbi Jeremiah Silverman always felt a bit invigorated on Mondays. The beginning of his workweek always seemed rife with possibilities for both good and bad, and that always had him on his toes and feeling alive. Occasionally it also left him frustrated because he couldn't choke the life out of someone who deserved it.

This particular Monday was starting out with a bang, and it wasn't a good one at that. Already Marie had lectured him on three separate topics, none of which seemed of the least importance to him, even though they seemed to represent the end of the world to her. Four members of his congregation had come in to complain about the forthcoming Halloween festivities at the church next door. A father had dragged his son in for counseling after the boy had told his parents he didn't want to be a grown up and therefore was going to refuse to participate in any Bar Mitzvah activities. Lastly was the fact that Cindy seemed to be angry with him and for the life of him he had no idea why.

So when his phone rang and he discovered Detective Mark Walters on the other end he wasn't sure whether to view it as a welcome respite or a natural progression of the morning's chaos.

"Detective, what can I do for you?" he asked. He knew that it upset Mark that he was using his title lately, but it was hard since the events that had happened in Israel to let down his guard enough to express the intimacy of friendship by calling the man by his first name.

"Rabbi," Mark growled, clearly in a worse mood than usual. "I have a bit of a problem and I find myself in need of your particular expertise. I need your professional opinion on something."

Jeremiah hesitated. It was also more than a bit awkward now that Mark knew that his previous employer had been the Mossad. Now he was truly unclear if Mark was hoping to talk to the rabbi or the assassin.

"Which professional opinion are you needing?" Jeremiah asked cautiously.

"Both of them," Mark said, sounding even more upset.

"That can't be a good thing."

"It isn't. It's probably one of the worst things I've seen in my entire career and I need you to get down here *now*."

"Alright, where are you?"

Mark gave him an address and Jeremiah wrote it down.

"Do you need me to bring anything?"

"Yeah. See if you can pick up one of the pastors from next door. I might need their opinion, too."

"What has happened?" Jeremiah asked, now growing alarmed.

"I can't explain it. You'll see for yourself when you get here."

Mark hung up the phone without saying anything else.

With a sigh Jeremiah got up from his desk. Whatever was going on, it couldn't be any crazier than things had been around there that morning.

"Are you okay?" Geanie asked as Cindy Preston slammed her desk drawer shut.

"Fine," Cindy grumbled.

Geanie snorted. "Really? That's the best you can do?"

Cindy turned toward her. "No, I'm not fine."

"Better. Care to tell me why?"

"The Halloween party," Cindy managed to spit out.

"Okay, the one here at the church or the one Joseph and I are throwing?" Geanie asked cautiously.

"The one at your guys' house," Cindy said.

"You have a problem with our Halloween party?" Geanie asked, sounding a bit bewildered and staring at her with huge eyes.

Cindy sighed and rubbed her forehead with her hand. "It's not that I have a problem with your party. I'm just having a problem because of your party."

"Okay, now you really need to explain," Geanie said.

"It's Jeremiah. I thought maybe we could coordinate our costumes."

"Do a couple costume, yeah, sure. And the problem is?"

"Not only is he not that into the idea of dressing up, but he also doesn't seem to be interested in choosing a costume that would be conducive to me wearing something to match."

"He doesn't want to do a couple's costume and you're mad at him for it," Geanie said, the light dawning in her eyes.

"Yes, well, no, but yes," Cindy said, frustration flooding her.

"Or are you more mad that you're not actually a couple?" Geanie guessed.

"I'm upset because things have been hard since we got back from overseas," Cindy said, still feeling cautious about mentioning that they were actually in Israel. Which in and of itself was weird. Everyone at Jeremiah's synagogue knew he'd been in Israel in July. They all thought he'd been dealing with family issues. And while they had dealt with family issues after all, that wasn't a good excuse for where Cindy had been and what she'd been doing. Most people knew that she'd had some sort of emergency in July and that's why she had disappeared, but only those close to them knew she'd been in Israel with Jeremiah helping to stop a terrorist plot.

Even then there was so much she wasn't allowed to talk about with other people. There had been a swarm of government agents for both Israel and America that had sworn her to secrecy in every way possible. Still, a few people at least knew something about the truth. Geanie knew more than most. After all, she was the only one Cindy had confided in about the kiss between her and Jeremiah. Kisses. There had been multiple.

Now that they were home, things were awkward, though. Jeremiah clearly didn't want to talk about what had happened in Israel and maybe that was how he coped with it, but she needed to be able to talk to him about everything that had happened. Since they'd been back they'd only kissed a handful of times, too, and usually when they did Jeremiah managed to have a guilty look on his face which just made her more upset.

They couldn't talk about Israel. They couldn't talk about them as a quasi-couple. Frankly, anything they could talk about was boring and shallow seeming in comparison. If she had one more polite meal with him she thought she might throw a fit.

Not that it was entirely his fault. Back home it had been easy to slip into old habits and see the events in Israel as a far-off dream at best or someone else's life at worst. She certainly hadn't been as outspoken or aggressive with him since their plane had touched down on U.S. soil.

She told herself that she was trying to give him space to re-acclimate to life as a rabbi instead of a spy. In reality she was scared that he had changed his mind about them and he didn't know how to tell her.

"Earth to Cindy."

Cindy realized she'd been completely lost in her own thoughts. "I'm sorry, Geanie, what were you saying?"

"I was asking what kind of costumes you wish you and Jeremiah were wearing."

"Something fun, maybe a bit romantic."

"Sexy?" Geanie asked.

Cindy was furious at herself for blushing when Geanie said the word. "A little wouldn't be bad, although I have a feeling you're probably going to take the prize in that category. What are you and Joseph dressing up as for the party?"

"Gomez and Morticia Addams."

"Why Gomez and Morticia?" Cindy asked.

"Because in my opinion they are one of the absolute sexiest screen couples," Geanie said with a grin. "Raul Julia and Angelica Houston were so hot together. The dialogue was amazing, the passion was tangible."

"Clearly I'm going to have to see the movies," Cindy said with a small chuckle. She had always admired Geanie's passion for things.

Geanie's eyes widened. "You mean you haven't?"

"No."

"How were we roommates for all those months and I never knew this? I would totally have made you watch them on movie night."

"Okay, now I'm curious who you think the other hot screen couples are," Cindy said with a laugh.

"My other fave is Batman and Catwoman in the Michael Keaton and Michelle Pfeiffer version. When she had him pinned on that roof and they had the discussion about mistletoe and kisses both being deadly and then she licked his face? I thought I might die."

Cindy laughed at the expression on Geanie's face. She couldn't help it. The other woman was so clearly enraptured by what she was saying. "I must say that I'm pretty fond of Zorro," she admitted after a few moments.

"Zorro's always good, very handsome and exciting. He was one of my heroes growing up. I used to love anything with him, the Lone Ranger, or Robin Hood," Geanie said. "So what kind of costumes has Jeremiah suggested?"

"Let's see, his first choice was rabbi," Cindy said, unable to contain the sarcasm in her voice.

Geanie winced. "I'm not sure what's worse, the idea that he's threatening to basically not dress up or that he thinks that the rabbi is a costume and not the real him."

Cindy went very still. She hadn't thought of that. She had just thought he was trying to get out of dressing up. It had never occurred to her that he could be having so many problems fitting back into this life that he saw the rabbi as a character he was putting on and not something real that was part of him. She felt suddenly very sad.

The door opened and she blinked in surprise as Jeremiah walked in.

"Speak of the devil," Geanie said softly.

Cindy could tell from the way Jeremiah's eyes flicked toward the other woman that he had heard her. He had frighteningly good hearing and she had only just recently started to figure out how good it really was.

She forced a smile on her face. "Are you here for lunch?" she asked.

It was a bit early, but she didn't know what else to think.

He shook his head. "Actually Detective Walters called and he wanted me to come down and give my opinion on a crime scene. He asked me to see if any of the pastors here were available to come as well."

"That sounds ominous," Geanie said.

Cindy couldn't help but agree. "Why does Mark want to see one of the pastors?" she asked.

"He didn't say, but I gather he wants a religious perspective on whatever it is he's run across."

"All of them are actually tied up the rest of the day," Cindy said.

"But you know, I'm sure Cindy could offer some religious perspective on it," Geanie said quickly.

Cindy was about to object. She was in no way as schooled in theology as a pastor. She did know more than Mark, though, and she found herself burning with curiosity. Plus, she had to admit that she wanted to spend some more time with Jeremiah. It was possible that she'd been overly harsh in her estimate of his costume choosing skills.

"I could certainly try," Cindy said. "I can take my lunch break now and go with you," she said, grabbing her purse and standing up.

"Yes, you two have fun solving crime," Geanie said brightly.

Cindy bit her lip to keep from saying something obnoxious. Jeremiah was staring at her oddly, but he wasn't objecting.

"Let's go," she said, heading for the door.

Once she was settled in the passenger seat of his car Cindy forced herself to take a deep breath, trying to flush out the hostility she had been feeling earlier. She smiled at Jeremiah as he put the car in drive.

"How are you doing?" she asked.

"It's been a busy morning. Marie just kept going on and on. I'm not even sure about what," he said with a sigh.

"I'm sorry to hear that, but I meant more in a big picture sort of way."

She could see a muscle clench in his jaw. Normally that would have been answer enough, but she pressed on. "It's been hard, not being able to talk about everything that happened," she said. "I know I can't talk about it with other people, but I was hoping you and I could at least discuss things."

"What do you want to discuss?" he asked.

"Everything. Anything. A lot changed a couple of months ago. For me. For you. For us."

"I know. I'm sorry."

"Don't apologize," she said, trying to keep the anger that flared up within her out of her voice. "I'm glad. I've grown so much as a person and I could never go back to being the scared child that I was when you first met me."

"You were hardly a child."

"Not in years, but I felt like one. Lost, alone, terrified of everyone and everything in the great big world. You set me free from that. I would not change it for anything in the world."

"You set yourself free," he told her.

"Even if I did, I couldn't have done so without you and God helping, pushing, encouraging."

She reached over and put her hand on his knee. Even that simple act caused her heart to start pounding and a part of her said that she was being too brazen, that she had no right to touch him like that.

But she had every right. He had given her the right. She remembered what he'd told her back in Israel, even if he had forgotten. He didn't say anything and she left her hand where it was. The intimacy felt forced, but she refused to budge.

"I need you," she said softly.

"I know," he said, with a slight catch in his voice. "I'm sorry I haven't been there for you. What happened, everything you've gone through. It had to have been traumatic."

"Life altering," she interjected.

"And you're right, I'm the person you need to talk to, should talk to, and I just haven't been ready to talk about any of it."

"I know, and I've tried to be patient, but things can get pretty noisy in my head when I've just got myself to talk to," she said, trying to keep her tone light.

He let go of the steering wheel with his right hand, and before she knew what he was going to do he had picked up her hand and kissed her fingers. Gently he set it back down and she felt a thrill of triumph when he put her hand back on his knee. What was the saying about victory being won in inches instead of miles?

She was content to let the rest of the ride pass in silence. As it turned out it was only a couple more minutes. Jeremiah turned onto a street that seemed vaguely familiar. All the houses were incredibly rundown, but none of them compared to the house at the end of the street. Weeds had overtaken the front yard and the glass panes in the windows were jagged and broken. There were steps leading up to the front porch and three were sagging, one was broken, and another was missing altogether.

The police cars parked outside were the only indication that there was life somewhere on the premises.

"Okay, this gets my vote for creepiest haunted house," Cindy said. She was trying to joke, but something about the structure, its walls stained a dark color that was nearly black and two dormer windows on the third floor staring like eyes, made her blood run cold. Her stomach twisted and she had a sudden, overwhelming urge to stay in the car.

She felt embarrassed by her unreasoning terror. Here she had been talking to Jeremiah about how much she'd grown and changed from the terrified creature she had once been and not ten minutes later she wanted to cower in the car while he went into the spooky house without her.

Snap out of it, she told herself sternly, as she pushed open the car door and forced herself to get out.

"This feels...wrong," Jeremiah muttered.

"I couldn't agree more," she admitted.

She would have asked him if he was sure they were in the right place, but the police cars spoke for themselves.

She even recognized Mark's car, but it was empty. All the officers had to be inside.

She walked around the car and grabbed Jeremiah's hand, trying to steady herself. He gave it a squeeze and together they started forward.

"Careful on these steps," he warned, as he began testing the bottom one before putting his weight fully on it. It groaned but it held.

She followed him up the stairs, putting her feet where he had. Earlier in the car her heart had been pounding in excitement and now it was pounding in fear. She could feel sweat start to bead on her forehead and her stomach twisted, cramping harder.

This is not a good place, she thought.

They made it up onto the porch and then crossed to the door which was gaping open and sagging slightly on its hinges.

"Hello?" Jeremiah called, clearly as unwilling to cross over the threshold as she was.

Hello.

Cindy jerked. "Did you hear that?" she asked. It had been faint, but close, like someone whispering in her ear.

Jeremiah shook his head, but he looked worried.

"Jeremiah?" she heard Mark call from inside a few seconds later.

She felt a bit of relief. At least he was here and okay, not swallowed up by the horrid house. She wiped the sweat off her forehead. The place was really getting to her. She had never liked desolate, abandoned places and this one was by far the creepiest she had ever seen.

She heard footsteps echoing inside and then saw a light bobbing up and down in the gloom. "Glad you could make it," she heard Mark say.

A second later she saw him, holding a flashlight, and crossing a dusty, cobweb filled entryway toward them. He paused slightly when he saw her and glanced at Jeremiah.

"No pastors?"

"No pastors," Jeremiah affirmed.

Mark let loose with a string of profanity unlike any she'd ever heard from him. They stepped back and made room for Mark to join them on the porch. She instantly noticed that he was drenched in sweat and his pupils were dilated.

"It's not good in there," he said tersely.

"You asked for religious expert opinions. Here we are," Jeremiah said.

Mark wiped his forehead on his shirt sleeve. "Creepy house," he muttered under his breath.

"What is going on here?" Cindy asked.

"I don't know, that's why I called," Mark admitted. He stared at her intently. "There's something...occult about all of this. Six months ago I wouldn't have let you anywhere near that basement, but a lot has changed. If you can't handle it, though, just say so."

Cindy swallowed hard. It was a test of the new her and she didn't want to fail. Nothing in her wanted to go into that house, but she didn't want to let Jeremiah or herself down. "I'm okay," she said, grateful that her voice at least sounded steady.

Jeremiah didn't want Cindy to have to put on a brave face and go see whatever the detective had called them out to see. He wanted to shield her from whatever horror waited. But he respected her resolve and he knew that he should let her go if that was what she had wanted. He tried to calm himself down. This was just another homicide, even if it was in a creepy house. It had been a crazy morning, how much worse could it get?

Mark turned and led the way into the house. They followed close behind, Cindy still holding onto his hand. He could hear floorboards creaking above him and he glanced up.

"I've got officers sweeping the rest of the house," Mark said as if sensing his sudden concern.

He led the way to the kitchen. Toward the back of it a door gaped open and he could see the start of a staircase heading down.

"Most California houses don't have basements," Cindy said.

"Yeah, well this isn't most California houses," Mark said grimly. "Stay close."

There was no electricity so they descended the stairs with only Mark's flashlight to guide them. Jeremiah kept swiveling his head, feeling like he was hearing soft noises, whispers that he couldn't quite pin down.

As they neared the bottom of the stairs Jeremiah could see more light and at last he could tell that it was coming from electric lanterns that had been set up to cast light on the scene. The lanterns looked powerful, but their light seemed to be swallowed up almost instantly by darkness. There were deep shadows everywhere and the light couldn't do enough to keep them at bay.

He felt Cindy clutch his hand tighter and he could hear her breathing. It was shallow, frightened sounding. When they made it down to the basement floor he felt a sick wrenching sensation in his gut. He could smell something, powerful, pungent. It wasn't blood, but he couldn't identify the smell. It gave him the overwhelming feeling of danger and he silently cursed himself for having left his gun in his office at the synagogue. He hadn't wanted to risk one of the church pastors seeing him carrying it.

"Something bad happened here," Cindy whispered, and he was inclined to agree with her.

Mark walked a bit farther and they followed until they could see what it was he was shining his flashlight on. He felt Cindy jerk to a stop and gasp. She started to shake as he just stared at the body on the ground.

It was a young woman, probably about twenty, if that. She had ritualistic markings all over her body. She was dead, eyes fixed and staring in a terror that communicated itself to him. There were no signs of physical trauma to the body, though, no obvious causes of death. Her arms were straight out at her sides, wrists bound by ropes which were secured at the other ends by a stake in the ground. Her legs were also bound and angled away from each other. Her entire body had been positioned and laid out in exact lines on top of the bloody pentagram she was staked out on top of.

"I was wrong," Jeremiah said softly to himself. "This is crazier."

2

Cindy wanted out of that basement badly. The hair on her neck and arms was all standing on end, and the sick feeling inside her stomach that she'd had outside the house intensified tenfold. This whole place was unnatural. Evil. The dark, the cold, and a faint, unpleasant odor all urged her to leave this place and never look back.

"What killed her?" Jeremiah asked softly.

The devil, Cindy thought, but managed not to say out loud.

"We won't know until the coroner can examine her. As you can tell there are no obvious signs of injury. It could be we're looking at poison or something like that."

Cindy didn't believe it. She should. She knew she should. It was logical, it made sense. The problem was, nothing else about what she was seeing and feeling made any sense. Her stomach cramped even harder, causing her to involuntarily bend over slightly which just brought her that much closer to the body.

Jeremiah stepped forward, and it took all of her strength to let go of his hand. Slowly he knelt down next to the body, head moving back and forth as he took in all the details.

An upside down pentagram was drawn in what looked like marker on the woman's forehead. That was the only symbol that she recognized.

"Some of these symbols are Hebrew. Others are from long dead cultures," Jeremiah said.

"How come you recognize some of the older ones?" Mark asked.

Jeremiah grimaced. "I had an...associate...who preferred using archaic means of communication."

"I knew both your careers would come in handy," Mark said quietly.

Cindy couldn't pry her eyes off the woman's body. Underneath the fear that she was feeling there was another emotion stirring. Anger. Someone had done something terrible to this woman, and it was clear she had died in terror.

Suddenly she felt a chill dance down her spine and she spun around, sure that she had heard a footstep behind her in the dark. There was no one there. At least, no one that she could see. The sick feeling in her gut intensified and she realized that she had started shaking uncontrollably.

"Can we get out of here?" She barely managed to get the words out around the sudden tightness in her throat. She couldn't breathe and it was almost as though she could feel fingers closing around her neck, squeezing, cutting off more and more of her air.

She took a step back toward the stairs as she heard her own breaths coming as ragged gasps. Her head was starting to swim, and she knew that she had to get out of there.

Something doesn't want us here, the thought came unbidden into her mind.

She saw Mark twist around suddenly as though he, too, heard something. His hand was on the gun under his jacket, and when he turned back the dim light reflected off the sweat that was coating his forehead.

Cindy took another step toward the stairs, hoping that it would make her feel better. Instead of the pressure on her throat easing up it only seemed to get worse. Her fingertips were tingling and her gasping breaths sounded thunderously loud in the dark.

Mark jerked around again, this time half-pulling his gun from his holster. She could hear Jeremiah muttering something to himself in Hebrew as he continued to stare at the body.

The room was beginning to swim before her eyes, and Cindy realized she was about to collapse. She tried to say something, to warn Jeremiah and Mark. They weren't alone, she could feel it. Something was watching them, and it didn't want them there.

Leave.

The words hung in the air, the faintest whisper of sound.

Cindy turned and grabbed the handrail. She hauled herself up five quick steps before the world began to tilt in front of her. She couldn't breathe, couldn't think. Her legs wouldn't do what she told them to do, and without knowing how it had happened she found herself tumbling backward.

She landed hard on her back on the cement floor, her feet caught up on the first step. She tried to grab her throat, but her arms wouldn't move. She tried to yell for help, but not even a whisper escaped her lips. She had lost feeling in her legs and everything was going black when she felt arms around her.

Jeremiah. She knew it was him even though she couldn't see him in the gathering darkness. He would protect her. She was safe. Still she knew that she had to do what she could to stay conscious.

A moment later she could feel herself being bounced around as they raced up the stairs. She could hear them creaking and groaning and for one terrible moment she thought they were going to crash through them. The wood held, though, and soon they were running through the house, then out onto the porch, then they were by the car.

She heard someone shouting, but she didn't think it was Jeremiah. The pressure on her throat was beginning to ease up and relief surged through her. They were out of the hideous house. Everything was going to be fine.

Someone came over and after a moment she realized it was a paramedic. She hadn't realized there were any there at the house. Jeremiah put her down on the ground, and the other man bent over her and began to examine her.

After looking her over he said, "You're having an allergic reaction to something."

She remembered the strange smell that had been in the basement and wondered if it could be connected.

"Are you allergic to anything that you know of?" he continued.

She shook her head, not sure if she could speak yet. He asked a couple of more questions and then gave her some medication. Faster than she would have thought possible she was able to start breathing freely again. With Jeremiah's help she sat up slowly, just in time to see the medical examiner bringing the body out of the house.

Mark exchanged a few words with both him and the paramedic before he came over.

"You doing okay?" he asked, worry evident in his tone.

"Yes," Cindy managed to say.

"You had us worried. I wonder what you were allergic to?"

She shook her head. She didn't know, but she hoped to never encounter whatever it was again.

"You might want to see a doctor and have the whole battery of allergy tests," he suggested.

It was probably a good idea. She shuddered to think what might have happened if she had been alone when the attack happened. Then again, there was no way she would have been alone in that house. Still, whatever was in it that had triggered the reaction could be something she might encounter elsewhere.

"It's a heck of a thing," Mark said, looking distracted.

"Where's Liam?" Cindy asked, realizing she hadn't seen Mark's partner.

"On vacation, lucky son-of-a-gun. Wish I was. In all my years I've never seen anything quite like this."

"Nor have I," Jeremiah offered.

"You said she had a mixture of symbols on her. What do the symbols mean?" Mark asked. "I mean, obviously pentagrams are Satanic."

Jeremiah shook his head slowly. "That one in particular was symbolic of evil because it was upside down and that would seem to be the intent of it. Regular ones with the single point facing upward aren't Satanic."

"What do you mean?" he asked.

"The normal pentagram is a Christian symbol representing the five wounds of Christ: head, both hands, and both feet. The upside down version didn't become a negative thing until more modern times when occultists and Satanists used it to represent something contrary."

Cindy had heard something like that before, though she couldn't remember where.

"So, point up okay, point down bad?" Mark asked. "That makes no sense."

"It's the inversion, the opposite. Like the difference between a cross and an upside down cross," Cindy said. She guessed even that was a corrupted symbol, though. Legend had it that the Apostle Peter had been crucified upside down because he didn't consider himself worthy to be killed in the same manner as Christ. Even an act of humility could be corrupted by those with evil intentions.

Jeremiah was still worried about Cindy. When she had fallen off the stairs it had scared him, and when he realized she wasn't breathing right he had felt a kind of powerlessness he never wanted to feel again.

There was something deeply wrong with the house and particularly the basement. He had been doing his best to try and block it out, even though his imagination had been working overtime. He could have sworn he'd heard noises, whispers, most inaudible but a few startlingly clear.

He had told himself that it was nothing, merely an old building and the suggestion of what had happened in it. The fact that both Mark and Cindy had been radiating their own fear hadn't helped any so he'd been trying to ignore that, too. Which was why he hadn't realized Cindy was in trouble earlier.

"If you get me photographs from the coroner of the symbols, I'll see what I can do to translate them for you," he said. He didn't want to admit it, but even though he'd known exactly what the Hebrew meant at the time he'd been staring at the body, he couldn't remember what it was. That also scared him. He'd never had problems with recall like that before. He wondered if the shock of Cindy falling had been great enough to cause him to forget or if there was something more at work. What he did know was that he was grateful to be out of that basement, and he wished that he'd never answered the phone when Mark had called that morning.

"I'll see that you get the pictures as soon as possible," Mark said. "I've got a bad feeling about this whole mess, and we need to get to the bottom of it fast. I'm sorry I pulled you two into this."

Jeremiah just nodded. It wouldn't do any good to echo the man's sentiment.

An officer approached Mark and Jeremiah noted that the man was pale. "We finished checking the rest of the house," he told the detective.

"And?" Mark asked tersely.

"We didn't find anything. It appears to be completely abandoned. No furniture, no signs of habitation. There were thick coats of dust on everything."

"Any chance there was a nice clear fingerprint in one of those layers of dust?" Mark asked.

"I'm sorry, sir."

"Of course. Why should any of this be easy?" Mark grumbled.

Jeremiah could tell the other man was still frightened, and he didn't blame him. He wouldn't want to be in his shoes right now. This investigation was going to turn ugly and both of them knew it. Given the nature of the crime and the way the body had looked, if the press got wind of it, then things would just get crazier.

Nobody needed that. Especially not this close to Halloween. It even had the potential to make national news which was a kind of nightmare none of them needed to live through.

Deep in his gut he felt that old, familiar urge to disappear. Attention was the last thing someone like him wanted. Nosy reporters and a national stage was one of the worst things that could happen. If it did explode into big news there'd be no way he'd be able to stay out of it. The very fact that he'd been here would send the reporters his way and they'd dig into his life, Cindy's life, everything.

"What's wrong?" Mark asked sharply. "Are you hurt?" He was staring down at Jeremiah's right hand.

Jeremiah glanced down and saw blood drops seeping out between his fingers. He'd clenched his fists so tight thinking about what might be coming that he'd dug his fingernails hard enough into his palm to make it bleed.

"It's nothing," he said, forcing himself to relax his hands.

Mark looked like he was about to argue, but just then another police officer called him over to look at something in the dirt. Jeremiah suspected it was probably some sort of tire track or shoe imprint. Whatever it was, he was grateful for the reprieve.

He looked at Cindy. The color had finally come back into her cheeks.

"We should take you to the hospital or a doctor to get checked out. We need to know what it is you're allergic to," he said.

"I just want to get out of here," she said, "but I'd rather go back to work or home."

He didn't argue with her even though he was worried. Too many strange things had happened in that basement that he couldn't explain. He wanted answers, but, even

22

more than that, he wanted reassurances about Cindy's health and information on how to avoid another emergency.

"Well, hopefully we can go soon," Jeremiah said.

As it was, both Mark and the paramedic insisted that Cindy go to the emergency room just to be checked out. Several hours later they were driving back to the church. Whatever the reaction had been to, the medication she had been given had taken care of things. She also had an appointment with her doctor later in the week to do the allergy tests to find out what it might have been that set her off. It wasn't ideal, but at least they would be getting some answers.

It was after six when they got back to the church parking lot. It was empty except for Cindy's car which was parked next to the building. Jeremiah pulled up next to it and she got out of the car, every line of her body telegraphing just how tired she was. He didn't blame her. It had been a traumatic day.

He got out as well and moved toward her car. She turned to look at the gate that led into the church courtyard and stopped, keys in her hand.

"What is it?" he asked.

"The gate's ajar. It should be locked. Last person to leave always locks up."

Normally he would have assumed that one of the pastors was working late, but there were no cars in the parking lot other than hers so he was instantly on guard.

He moved toward the gate, waving at Cindy to stay put. He could feel her moving closer, though. He pushed the gate open wide enough for them to pass through. He looked for any lights on in the buildings, but the only illumination was coming from the exterior lights.

They were nearing one of the corners of the building closest to the parking lot when he heard a soft step coming toward them. He froze, tensing his muscles. Someone was there. It wouldn't be the first time criminals had trespassed on church property. He waited, holding his breath as he listened to the footsteps approaching.

A form flashed into sight. Jeremiah lunged out, reaching for the man in front of him.

3

Jeremiah was reaching for the man's throat when he recognized him. He pulled back at the last second as Dave Wyman shouted in terror. The youth pastor, who everyone called Wildman, scrambled backward several feet and then stood, staring at him as though he had just seen a ghost.

"I'm sorry, you startled us," Jeremiah said with a grimace. "We thought you were an intruder."

"I startled you?" Wildman asked, voice cracking slightly.

Cindy moved to join them. "Are you okay?" she asked.

"No, I'm not," Wildman said. "You nearly scared me to death."

Before Jeremiah could respond Wildman stepped forward and grabbed his shoulders. Jeremiah struggled not to shrink back at the contact or respond in some other inappropriate way. He'd barely managed not to knock the man out already once today.

"Do you know what this means?" Wildman asked, his eyes getting even wider.

Jeremiah didn't and he wasn't sure he wanted to. He forced himself to shake his head.

"This is fantastic! I've been having problems explaining to the kids who are going to be running the haunted house here at the church how to scare people. You could show them!"

"What do you mean?"

"We could run a workshop, either after school or on the weekend and you could teach them how to scare people as badly as you scared me."

"That was an accident," Jeremiah said quickly. "I don't know the first thing about scaring people."

It was a lie, but the ways in which he frightened people were most certainly not the kind of thing that the pastor was looking for and certainly wouldn't work for a haunted house type attraction.

"Come on. The kids look up to you, they respect you. They still talk about the hero rabbi who saved them all at Green Pastures."

Jeremiah forced himself not to react outwardly to that news. He didn't like that he was notorious for that. No matter what he did it seemed he was having an increasingly hard time keeping a low profile, and keeping his skills a secret, in this community.

"I just did what you or any of the other adults would have done," Jeremiah said evenly.

"Um, sure, keep telling yourself that," the pastor said with a dusting of sarcasm in his voice.

"Just do it," Cindy said quietly.

Jeremiah glanced at her. "You want me to teach a bunch of kids how to better scare people?"

She nodded.

"Fine," he said with a sigh. He could show up, try to show them one or two scare tactics and then Wildman would stop talking about it.

"This is going to be epic," the pastor said with a grin of insane joy.

His phone chimed and he pulled it out of his pocket. He glanced at it and then grimaced. "Well, at least there was some good news today."

"What's wrong?" Cindy asked.

"My car's been in the shop all day and it won't be ready until tomorrow. I'll have to call a taxi."

"I can drop you home," Cindy volunteered.

Jeremiah thought she was going crazy. She already looked completely exhausted and he figured she'd be eager to get home as quickly as possible. The noble thing to do would be to offer to drive Wildman instead, but Jeremiah was not eager to continue the Green Pastures line of conversation.

"Are you sure?" Wildman asked, perking back up.

She nodded. "You're not that far from my house."

"Fantastic! I've got some more Halloween plans I'd like to run by you," he said.

"Okay. Jeremiah, I'll see you later," she said, giving him a wan smile.

He stepped forward to hug her, but then checked himself. They weren't being demonstrative in that way in front of other people. He thought he caught a look of disappointment in her eyes when he stopped short.

"I'll see you tomorrow," he said.

Together they walked out to the parking lot and the pastor locked the gate after they had exited. Jeremiah felt a little unsettled as he watched Dave get into Cindy's car. He felt a pang of jealousy which was completely absurd. Even as he tried to dismiss it he couldn't help but try to remember if he'd ever heard anything about the pastor being married.

"I could swear Jeremiah looks angry with me," Dave said as Cindy started the car.

She glanced out her window but Jeremiah was getting into his own car and she couldn't see his face. "He's probably just still on edge," she said. She didn't mention that she was sure he wasn't happy about teaching the kids how to better scare people. She knew Wildman wasn't about to let that one go, though, so she'd urged him to do it. In the end it would be easier than trying to explain why he didn't want to. Persistence was one trait that many youth pastors shared in common and Dave had an overabundance of it. Sometimes he was worse than a little kid in that regard. He just would not let things go.

"No, I don't think that's it," he said thoughtfully. "I think he's upset that you're giving me a ride."

"That's ridiculous," Cindy replied. "Why on earth would that upset him?"

"If I had to guess I'd say because he likes you and he doesn't want other guys around."

"I don't think Jeremiah is jealous," Cindy said, struggling to control an eye roll. The very idea was preposterous. There was no need for him to be jealous of anyone, let alone Dave.

"I wouldn't be so sure," the pastor said. "And speaking of Jeremiah, what is the deal with you two anyway?"

"What do you mean?"

"Don't play coy. You know what I mean. You like him. He likes you. What's going on with that?"

Cindy was on the verge of saying "nothing", but at the last moment changed her mind. "I don't know," she admitted.

"You might want to figure it out before one of you explodes," he said.

"It's...complicated."

"I get that, but still, the way you're dancing around each other must be crazy making. Like, date already."

"Why are you pushing this?"

"Because I like you both and I think you're good for each other even though there are some issues clearly in your way."

"Really?"

"Yes, and if someone tells you it's because I said you'd be a couple by Halloween in the unofficial office betting pool, don't believe them."

"There's a bet going on about when Jeremiah and I are going to get together?"
Cindy asked, aghast.

"Yes, but don't tell anyone I told you. Strictly speaking that's against the rules."

"That's horrible! I can't believe you guys are betting on that!" She couldn't help but feel offended and even a tiny bit like her privacy was being violated.

"Don't be mad," Wildman said gently. "Instead take it as a sign that what's between you and Jeremiah is real and so obvious that it seems like you're meant to be together. Everyone thinks so."

"Sure, everyone thinks so now," she grumbled. "But what will it be like if I actually said I was dating him? How many people would give me the unevenly yoked lecture?"

"Probably a lot. I do believe, though, that God has pulled the two of you together for a reason. He works in mysterious ways and sometimes has to do extraordinary things to get our attention. You guys worked next door to each other for how long and never once interacted?"

"You're saying God wanted me to trip over that dead body in the sanctuary so that Jeremiah and I could meet and then what?"

"I don't know. Only He does. Well, and maybe Jeremiah does, too."

"I think he might be more lost than I am on that issue," Cindy said before she could stop herself.

"You might just need to be patient with him. Sometimes guys can be stupid and slow, but we usually get there in the end."

"I actually don't know what to do," Cindy confessed. It was odd. She hadn't been planning on discussing Jeremiah with Dave. If anything she should be talking to Geanie or Joseph. Then again Dave knew them both but wasn't necessarily in their inner circle. Maybe he could be more objective and offer a little perspective the others couldn't.

"I know he has feelings for me. He's said so. But he's just been acting so distant."

"I don't know what happened when you guys were overseas visiting his family, but whatever it was it seems to have really shaken him up. Maybe he's just trying to get a little stability and sense of normalcy back in his life before stirring everything up again. Maybe he needs that to feel safe and to take on other challenges. You think you're worried about what people are going to say to you? Put yourself in his shoes. He's a rabbi, the spiritual head of his synagogue. You don't think people are going to have some words for him about dating outside his religion?"

"I know Marie will be thrilled," Cindy said, unable to keep the sarcasm out of her voice.

Dave made a good point. As much as she wasn't looking forward to the criticism, it would likely be ten times harder on Jeremiah. With everything he'd been through in Israel, she knew that he was still having trouble fitting back into his old life and acting like the rabbi everyone thought they knew. Maybe he was concerned that if someone actually confronted him about dating her that he'd say or do something that he shouldn't and cause worse problems for all of them.

"Why does life have to be so hard?" she sighed.

"I don't know, but it could be a lot worse. At least you have someone that you know cares for you. A great many people would give a lot for that."

"Dave, I'm sorry, I didn't think."

"I'm not talking about me. I was thinking about some of my kids. They have parents who don't care or can't be bothered to show it. Some of them don't even know where one or both of their parents are. They'd kill to have someone tell them they were special and loved. Heck, sometimes it feels like that's all I do week in and week out is tell them that they're special to God and that He loves them. I just keep hoping that they'll believe it, feel it, accept it, you know. And they want to, desperately, but some of them have been so burned. And these are the kids that are making it to church somehow, think of all those who aren't."

"There must be a lot of lost and hurting kids out there," Cindy said, feeling sorrow for them.

"There are. I see it every day and it breaks my heart. That's one of the reasons I've been so desperate for years to do this Halloween event."

"I don't follow."

"I know, I'm a Halloween junkie. I love the holiday almost as much as Geanie does. But I didn't want to do this maze for me. I didn't even want to do it for the kids who are already in the church. I wanted to do it for their friends and classmates who are so lost with no one to turn to. For many of them it will be their first time stepping foot on church ground, and I want the experience to be a fun, exciting one for them filled with laughter and fellowship and a sense of belonging. It's hard to be unchurched and try to change that. It's scary. You don't know the people, the culture, the rituals, anything. It's easier not to go even if you're curious, even if you're searching. This way they'll have been to a church even if it was only for an event. They'll have met kids who go here so they know that if they want to come back there will be familiar faces who will accept them. Perhaps in the end that human need to belong somewhere is one of the greatest needs that drives us."

"When I stop this car remind me to hug you," Cindy said, struggling not to start crying. As he had been talking her thoughts had actually gone to the young woman whose body she'd seen earlier. Had a desire to belong led to her falling in with the wrong people and getting killed? The thought was devastating.

"Okay, but just one hug, and don't tell Jeremiah," Dave teased, his voice suddenly lighthearted again.

Cindy shook her head. His ability to switch moods was something she could never hope to understand let alone match. She cleared her throat. "So, how can I help make this Halloween event one that will be legendary?"

She glanced at Dave and saw him grinning from ear to ear. "Oh believe me, I have a few ideas."

"I thought you might," she said, finding herself smiling back.

Mark had managed not to go back inside the creepy house once Cindy and Jeremiah left. He was still freaked out by it and even more so by what had happened to Cindy in the basement. The oddest thing was that just before she fell off the stairs he could swear he'd heard someone whispering at them to get out. Worse than that, though, he'd turned to watch her climb the stairs and from where he'd been standing he could have sworn that it looked like she didn't fall but that she was pushed.

Which was impossible. No one had been down there but the three of them. The stairs were empty except for her. There was no way someone could have pushed her. Not unless they were invisible.

Or dead.

A chill danced up his spine as he tried to shove the thought aside. He didn't believe in stuff like that. He was the logical one, the practical one. Superstitions and ghost stories were just that, a bunch of made up stuff people used to scare each other with.

Still, he wouldn't have gone back down in that basement today for anything. Finally they wrapped the entire place in police tape, and he was able to head home, more tired than he'd been in quite a while. It had been a desperately long day and all he wanted was to get home, kiss his family, have some dinner, and collapse.

Family. The word was still strange and new to him even though the twins were now three months old. He caught himself smiling just thinking about them. He was enjoying being a father more than he'd ever imagined. He also found himself worrying now more than he'd ever imagined, but he figured it was the cost of all the fun parts.

He finally turned onto his street and a few seconds later was parked in the driveway. He walked inside, hung his keys on the hook, and started to take off his coat. He froze in mid-movement as he caught sight of Traci standing in the kitchen facing him, arms folded over her chest. She looked upset and warning bells went off in his head. The worst of it was he couldn't figure out what she might be upset over. He quickly ran down a mental list of all the things he'd been expected to do in the last couple of days and couldn't think of anything he might have done or forgotten to have done to inspire that look.

"What is it?" he asked.

Traci continued to glare at him. "We need to talk."

4

Mark had often thought that *we need to talk* had to be the four scariest words in the English language. He finished taking his coat off as he felt himself beginning to panic.

"Okay, what's going on?" he asked, dragging the words out as though he were somehow trying to delay her pending answer. Truth be told he'd be happy never hearing the answer to his question.

"You have been avoiding the topic for seven days. Every night I try and talk about it and every night you ignore me completely. That's not going to happen again. Tonight you're going to talk and you're going to listen and we'll keep at it until we have a solution."

Now he was really scrambling as he tried to figure out what on earth she might be talking about. Whatever it was, it couldn't be good. As much as it pained him to say it he finally admitted, "I don't know what you're talking about."

"Oh, suddenly you don't know," she said.

He could tell that had only pushed her buttons more. He had to admit some of the hormonal changes she'd undergone in the aftermath of pregnancy had made his usually even-tempered wife more than a little unpredictable and occasionally hotheaded. Unfortunately, this seemed to be one of those times, and he was pretty sure there was nothing he could say that was going to make this any better.

"I'm sorry, Hon, I just don't understand," he said, wincing inwardly as he waited for her to lose it completely.

"No, clearly you don't. If you understood then you'd know that this is important to me. I don't want to make the wrong decision here and screw up one of the most important things in our children's lives."

"And that is...?"

"Their first Halloween party."

"The twins?" he asked, feeling even more unclear on what was happening.

"No. Geanie and Joseph."

He blinked at her for a moment and then everything finally clicked into place. "That's right, you mentioned that they were throwing a costume party."

"Not just a costume party, their first party that they're hosting as a married couple. First party. First costumes for the twins. We'll be showing pictures for years. This is huge. And you have ignored me every time I've tried to figure out what couple costume we should put together."

"I'm sorry. I just haven't known what to say."

"That's no excuse. You should try to contribute to the conversation. At least listen to and comment on my suggestions."

"Fair enough. What costumes have you thought of?"

"Remember that cotton candy girl who got trapped in The Zone a year or two ago and was chased all around by a serial killer? I was thinking we could do that."

"Serial killers are not my idea of a fun costume. Besides, too close to my job."

"Okay, something more historical, like Bonnie and Clyde."

Mark wrinkled his nose. "I'd really prefer not to be a bad guy."

She raised an eyebrow, but didn't comment.

"Austin Powers and a Fembot."

"While I think you'd look smashing, let's leave the spy stuff to Jeremiah. For all we know he's going as James Bond and I wouldn't want to compete with that."

"He *is* James Bond and there would be no competition," Traci said tartly.

Mark winced inwardly, but held his tongue.

"Beauty and the Beast."

It was one of Traci's favorite movies so he wasn't terribly surprised by the suggestion. Still, he didn't want to dress up like the Beast. After all, it had taken him months to get over feeling like a monster not that long ago. "The big head and fur suit would be too hot and I know you don't think he's nearly as attractive when he's the prince," he said.

"True. Alright, you suggest something," she said.

"The Lone Ranger and Tonto?"

"Only if I get to be the Lone Ranger. I don't want to be your sidekick."

Mark sighed, deciding he'd get nowhere trying to argue that Tonto was a partner and not a sidekick. "Okay, Batman and Catwoman."

"If the Beast costume is going to be too hot, the Batman one would be, too."

She had him there.

"So, you seem to be kicking around crime fighter type ideas," she commented.

"Yes. I'd like to go as a cop, but you already told me last time we went to a costume party that wasn't going to happen."

"That's right. Still, there's got to be something…I've got it! Dick Tracy," she said triumphantly.

Mark actually liked that idea. "Then you could go as Breathless Mahoney."

She narrowed her eyes. "Why not Tess Trueheart, his wife and one true love?"

Mark allowed his eyes to drift downward a bit. "Because I don't know how long you're going to be this size, but I'd like to take advantage of it and show off."

She blinked and then turned red. "Are you talking about my chest?"

"Absolutely."

She folded her arms over her chest with deliberate motions. "Tell you what, I'm the one named Traci. I'll go as the detective and you can go as Breathless."

"Um, no. You're not getting me into a dress."

"Wanna bet?" she asked, an edge to her voice.

Mark took a deep breath. "Sweetheart. I'm a guy, and I appreciate your current...enhancements...you can't blame me for that. I've been dying to see what you'd look like in a slinky dress. You're the most beautiful woman in the world and given that this is such an important party I want to make sure that you are the center of attention because you deserve to be."

He paused, hoping that what he'd said was the right thing. He watched her face closely for a sign of what she was thinking. Slowly the corners of her mouth began to turn up and he felt a flare of hope that this conversation might have a happy ending after all.

"You think I'm the most beautiful woman in the world?"

"Of course I do. I always have. And being a mother has given you even more of a radiance, a glow to you. You take my breath away."

She grinned. "And that's exactly why you should be Breathless."

He groaned, but inwardly he was relieved. She was teasing now and that was a good thing.

"Well, at least we know one of us will be Dick Tracy and the other of us will be either a femme fatale or a true blue heroine."

"That works."

Traci's smile slowly vanished and he braced himself as he wondered what was coming next.

"Are you okay? You look pale," she said.

He shook his head slowly. "It's been a rough day."

"How rough?"

"One of the worst."

Suddenly her face was filled with sympathy and she threw her arms around him. "I'm sorry, Sweetie," she said, her voice a little choked up. Her emotions really were close to the surface these days and they could change in the blink of an eye. "Do you want to talk about it?"

"I think I need to, but I don't want you to have to hear about it."

"Nonsense, that's part of my job. Hello, cop's wife." She pulled away and gave him a big smile. "Why don't we eat dinner and you can tell me all about it?"

"Okay."

He walked over and sat down at the kitchen table and it took all his willpower not to just put his head down on the table and fall asleep. Today was a day he was eager to be done with.

Traci pulled two plates out of the oven where she'd been keeping them warm. He frowned. It must be later than he'd thought.

"How are the kids?"

"Asleep."

"What?"

She gave him a pitying look as she set the plates down on the table. "It's after eight," she said.

He groaned. "No wonder I feel like I'm going to die."

"If it's any consolation, you look like you already did."

"Thanks," he said, too weary to even put the sarcasm into his voice.

She set two glasses of water down on the table before joining him. "So, what happened to you today?"

"The facts or what I'm worried is the answer?"

"What you're worried about first. Facts later."

"I think some sort of coven performed a ritual involving human sacrifice."

"What?" Traci asked, eyes bulging. She had picked up her water glass and she held it in mid-air, forgetting to bring it to her lips, as she stared at him. "You're kidding me, right?"

"I wish I was."

"Okay. I think I'm going to need the facts now."

Despite his best intentions Mark found himself describing the scene for her in detail. It was like it was burned into his memory and he couldn't stop himself from revealing all the horror to her. When he got to the part about Cindy looking like she'd been pushed down the stairs Traci actually gasped and jerked. The water from the glass she was still holding sloshed on her hand and she put it down, but didn't bother to try and clean up.

When he finished she just stared at him for a moment before reaching over and taking his hands in hers. "I don't want you going back there," she said, her voice shaking.

"I'm right there with you," he said.

"No, Mark, I'm serious. I've got a terrible feeling about all of this. Please, promise me you won't go back to that house."

In all the years they'd been married, all the years he'd been a cop investigating dangerous people, she had never once looked at him like this. She had never begged him not to do something.

"Traci, I can't promise that. I'm probably going to have to go back at least once."

"Don't, please," she whispered. Tears shimmered in her eyes and a moment later began to roll down her cheeks.

He stared at her in shock. He knew that the post-pregnancy hormones had made her more emotional, but this was something else. "Traci, it's my job," he said, at a loss as to what was going on with her.

"I know. I just don't want you to get killed over it."

"I'm not going to."

"You can't promise me that, and you know it as well as I. I'm telling you, Mark, I have a really awful feeling about this. There's something not right at work, and whatever it is, I don't want it coming anywhere near you. I couldn't stand to lose you. I couldn't."

He could feel himself starting to choke up a bit. His exhaustion coupled with her raw emotion was bringing it on.

"Traci, I've faced serial killers, and a lot of other scary things, and I've always been fine."

"Not this time. I can't tell you how I know, I just know that getting involved in this is a mistake."

He lifted their hands and kissed hers. "Come on, this doesn't sound like my Tess Trueheart. You should be telling me to go get the bad guys, that I'm smarter than they are and right will always win out."

"Maybe I am Breathless then, because no fight for justice is worth risking your life," she countered.

He took a deep breath. They needed to find a way to get past this so they could have some peace. "I promise you that I'll do everything I can to avoid going back in that house. The crime scene guys took a ton of pictures and that should be enough. Besides, I'll never forget the things I saw in there. Not if I live to be a hundred. Okay?"

After a moment she nodded. "Okay," she whispered, licking her lips. She took her hands back and wiped the tears from her cheeks. "Dinner's getting cold."

Neither of them had eaten while he had been telling her about what had happened. "It's fine," he said, forcing a smile as he picked up a fork and dug into his stroganoff.

The food was cold, but he didn't want any more interruptions to dinner. He wolfed it down, noticing that she barely ate a bite. He wanted to urge her to eat, but he was afraid to say anything at that point to her that might reopen the conversation.

He was almost done eating when the house phone rang, startling both of them. It was late for it to be any kind of good news. Traci jumped up from the table and grabbed it. His shoulders tensed up as he waited to hear who was on the other line.

"Hey, Amber," she said.

Mark relaxed. Amber was Traci's older sister. She and her husband were nice people. They had twins as well. It should have raised the red flag that it could be a possibility for him and Traci. As it turned out their own twins had been a surprise. Mark went back to finishing up his meal. His thoughts drifted to his nice soft bed and he couldn't wait to turn in and put this day behind him. Tomorrow he could start fresh.

"No, she doesn't talk to me anymore, not since I tried to talk to her about her life choices," Traci said.

They had to be talking about their youngest sister, Lizzie, who had chosen a while back to be wiccan and had gradually grown more hostile in general and had eventually shut Traci out when she tried to reach out to her. Mark kept telling Traci that one day Lizzie would come out the other side and they could reconnect with her then. It wasn't that he thought there was necessarily anything wrong with being wiccan, but it had been sold to him as a hippie type religion. Love people, heal the earth, do good, etc. Lizzie had definitely not been embracing the whole light and joy aspects last time he'd seen her.

"What do you mean?" Traci asked, her voice taking on an edge that got his attention. Whatever was going on it seemed to involve Lizzie and it didn't sound very good. Then again, Lizzie and trouble always had seemed to go hand-in-hand.

"Are you sure? Well, what should we do?"

Whatever was happening now sounded worse than usual. Mark knew he should care, but he'd gotten used to there being drama where Lizzie was concerned, and frankly he had a lot more to worry about.

"Oh no! Do that. Of course I will. I can check with some of her friends. I know she always used to hang around a couple of places, I'll check there, too. We might have to call the police."

Now Lizzie and her problems had his undivided attention.

What's going on? he mouthed to Traci who just shook her head slightly. She'd tell him later. Still, he got to his feet. He had the unsettling feeling that action was going to be called for the minute she got off the phone.

"Okay, okay. Bye."

Traci hung up the phone and turned to look at him. The color had drained out of her face.

"What's happened?"

"Lizzie hasn't been in her apartment for a week. Her roommate called Amber because she's getting worried."

Mark shook his head. "What are you saying?"

"My sister is missing."

5

After eating dinner Jeremiah decided to take Captain, his German Shepherd, to the park for a late night jog. He was keyed up from the day and needed to burn off some energy before he would have a chance at getting some sleep. After just a short car ride they were there, and Captain bounded excitedly next to him as he hit the jogging trail that ringed the park.

As they ran he kept replaying the day's events over in his mind. Mark had told him that it almost looked like Cindy had been pushed when she was on the stairs. They had both agreed that was impossible. Still, there were a lot of things that had happened that he didn't have an instant explanation for and that made him uneasy.

Off in the distance he saw flickering lights that seemed to be moving about. It was probably a group of bicyclists. Not wanting to be disturbed he turned and cut through the center of the park before picking up the jogging trail on the other side.

Cindy's allergy attack had scared him badly, and he realized he was still shaken up about it. Sometimes it seemed like his purpose in life, certainly the one that he clung to, was to keep her safe. How could he protect her from something like that, especially when the cause was unknown? He just hoped that when she went to the doctor they were able to discover the cause.

Suddenly he could feel Captain tensing beside him. It was amazing how in sync he and the dog had become. Jeremiah glanced at him and saw that Captain's ears were back and his teeth were bared. Jeremiah came to a halt and the dog pressed against his leg.

Jeremiah reached down to stroke his head, noticing that the dog's shoulder muscles were bunched tightly. A low rumbling came from his chest.

"What is it, boy?" Jeremiah asked softly.

Captain growled again.

Jeremiah turned and took stock of their surroundings. They seemed to be alone in this section of the park and behind them he didn't see the lights anymore. He reached out with his senses, trying to figure out what Captain was seeing or smelling that was making him uneasy. There was nothing, though, that he could tell.

"Time to go," Jeremiah said, angling across the park on the shortest route to the car. Captain kept pace with him, head swiveling constantly. They were almost there when the hair on the back of Jeremiah's neck stood up suddenly.

He stopped and turned quickly, half thinking there was someone behind him. Only darkness met his probing eyes, but the feeling of being watched intensified. Captain growled loudly and the sound ruptured the silence. The effect was to put Jeremiah even more on edge.

He turned even though every instinct told him that he was turning his back to danger. There was nothing he could detect, though. He forced himself to make it the last little way to the car. Once inside he locked the doors and waited for a moment, half-expecting to see a figure emerge from the darkness.

Nothing.

And that unnerved him like few other things could.

"I'm being paranoid," he said out loud. He couldn't make himself believe it, though. He knew, he felt in his gut, there was something lurking in the darkness that could see him even if he couldn't see it.

Mark was standing in the middle of his sister-in-law's bedroom trying to figure out what he was doing there. Her roommate, Michelle, was standing in the doorway looking anxious.

"It's been a week since you've seen Lizzie?" he asked.

She nodded, a lock of purple hair falling into her eyes.

"And how long have you gone without seeing her before?"

"Two, three days at the most."

There were no obvious signs of a struggle in the room. "Was there any suspicious activity, unlocked doors, tipped over furniture, strangers lurking around?"

"Not that I've seen."

"So, what makes you think something happened to her and she's just not on vacation or she met a new guy or something?" It was the politest way he could think to phrase it. He had volunteered to come over and check things out, although the look that Traci had given him before he left the house he had translated as "go over there or die". Now that he was here he was both relieved and frustrated to discover that there really wasn't anything to see.

He opened her closet and saw clothes hanging in neat rows. "Does she have a suitcase she normally uses when she's going to be away?"

"I'm not sure," Michelle admitted. "But she would have told me if she was going to be gone."

He closed the door and turned to look at her. "Were the two of you close?"

He winced when he realized he had used the past tense, making it sound like Lizzie was dead. *Too many years of interviewing friends and families of murder victims.*

"Not overly."

"Would she have told you if she was in some sort of trouble?"

"I don't know. I would hope so."

Mark nodded his head. The real answer was probably not. Most people got amazingly tight-lipped when they should be telling everyone that they thought they were in trouble.

"What about her coven? Maybe one of them would know where she is."

Michelle shrugged. "I don't know."

"Do you have a name or phone number for any of the other members?"

"No, she was always really weird, paranoid almost, about talking about the others. She would never say anyone's name but she'd call them different things if she wanted to talk about one of them."

"What would she call them?"

"Creepy tall guy, sweaty fat dude, sweater girl, trust fund brat, freaky eyes."

"Freaky eyes?" Mark questioned.

"Yeah, apparently they were some weird color, although I'm not sure what."

"And she talked about these people a lot?"

"Yeah, she hasn't talked about sweaty fat dude or sweater girl for a while, but the other three all the time."

"What else would she say about her coven?"

"Not a lot. She was pretty tight-lipped. I mean, in the beginning she would gush about how wonderful it was and all the cool things she could do. She kept trying to get me to go to one of their meetings or circles or whatever."

"Did you?"

"No way. I was not into that," Michelle said emphatically.

"So when did she start talking less about what they did?"

"Gosh, almost two years, I guess. Somewhere in there."

"Anything else happen at that time?" Mark asked.

"She had broken up with the guy she was dating and she was pretty upset. She was constantly raving that he was going to get what was coming to him and that no one could treat her that way and get away with it. Honestly, she started freaking me out."

"Then why didn't you move out?"

"Because I can't afford a place on my own and I didn't want her to catch me looking for a new roommate in case she'd somehow accuse me of betraying her then. Just when it was getting really bad, though, it all of a sudden stopped. That's when she became a lot quieter and didn't talk about the circles and the things they did even though she still mentioned some of the people. I was just relieved that she seemed to have gotten over it or whatever."

"What was her boyfriend's name?" Mark asked.

Michelle shook her head. "She always just called him by nicknames, like my sweetie or jerk face."

"Helpful," Mark said with a sigh. "You say you don't actually know the names of any of her coven members. Do you have any idea where they held their meetings?"

Michelle nodded. "She told me, in case I ever decided to drop by. They hold them in the park downtown near the really tall Redwood tree. They liked to be outdoors as long as the weather held."

"Do you know when these meetings occurred?"

"I know for a long time they met at least twice a month. They liked to meet on the nights of the full moon and the new moon. Lately, though, it seemed like she'd been going more often, maybe once a week, but I'm not sure on what day. It seemed to vary."

"Okay, can you show me which bathroom was hers?"

Michelle nodded and he followed her out of the room and to the bathroom just down the hall.

"This one is Lizzie's. I have my own," Michelle offered.

After a quick thirty second inspection Mark relaxed. He should have started with this room first and it would have saved him a lot of time.

"I don't think there's anything to worry about," he said.

"Why?"

"There's no toothbrush or toothpaste. Wherever she is, she planned to be gone."

Uncertainty flickered across Michelle's face. In that moment it was easy to see her real concern and unease over the entire situation.

"She'll probably turn up in a couple of days and tell you all about her little vacation," Mark said.

Slowly Michelle shook her head. "I don't think so," she murmured.

"Why not?"

The girl hesitated, biting her lower lip for a moment. Finally she answered him. "I've got this bad feeling, like in the pit of my stomach. I keep thinking something's wrong and that she's in danger. Last night I had a dream that...it doesn't matter."

"Do you often get these kinds of bad feelings?" Mark asked, watching her expression closely.

"Not very often, but when I do...I've never been wrong," she said, fear flickering in her eyes.

As a detective Mark had learned long ago to trust his gut. Sometimes you couldn't explain how or why you knew something, you just did. Since he'd had those experiences he was always loathe to dismiss it when others told him that they felt something in their gut. Sometimes they were wrong, but it never hurt to pay attention.

He reached out and put his hand on her shoulder. She jerked slightly and for a split second he felt like his hand was tingling.

"I'll do what I can to find her," he said.

Michelle nodded.

He removed his hand and got a business card out of his pocket. He handed it to her. "If you think of anything or hear anything, call me right away, any hour. Understood?"

"Yes," she said as she took the card.

"We will find her," he reaffirmed.

"Thank you."

When he left a minute later he wasn't entirely sure what to think. All he really knew was that he'd be no good to anyone if he didn't go home and get some sleep. He called Traci and filled her in. No need to keep her waiting and worrying while he drove home. She sounded slightly relieved when he told her about the missing toothbrush and he intentionally omitted Michelle's gut instinct that something was wrong. Given how strongly Traci had reacted earlier to hearing about his latest case he didn't want to add fuel to the fire of her worry. At least, not until he was convinced that they actually had something to worry about.

Like most people Cindy had never been a fan of needles, but she had been able to tolerate them. After today she was sure she never wanted to see another needle again for as long as she lived. After explaining to her doctor what had happened to her the day before she had been subjected to several dozen needle pricks all over her back with various possible allergens on them.

Now she was laying on her stomach, waiting for the doctor to return and tell her what she was allergic to. There had to be something because she did feel a distinct itchy sensation on one part of her back and another spot felt like it was on fire. Finally the door opened and the doctor came in.

Cindy waited impatiently while he examined her. After what seemed like forever he cleaned her back with some cotton balls dipped in alcohol.

"Okay, you can go ahead and put your shirt on. I'll be back in a couple of minutes to discuss the results," he said.

As soon as the door had closed Cindy put her clothes back on. A minute later he was back, chart in hand.

"The good news is, you don't appear to have many allergies. In fact there were only two things you reacted to. You had a minor reaction to ragweed. That's pretty common. The other reaction you had was much more significant and it was to acacia."

"Acacia? As in the tree?"

"Yes, it's an invasive species and is far more prevalent in the San Francisco Bay Area, but you can find it several places along the coast."

"When I had the allergy attack or whatever it was yesterday we were in a basement," Cindy said.

"It's possible it was growing outside and that you were exposed on your way in. Some cultures also burn it as incense."

"Are you sure that's it?" she asked.

"I'm fairly confident. You had a very strong reaction to it just now. The ragweed reaction wasn't strong enough to cause an incident like what you're describing, but it's possible the acacia could have. We could do another battery of tests, delving more into food allergies and the like, but you said you hadn't eaten for several hours before the attack and that you ate what you usually do at breakfast."

She nodded.

"I'm going to prescribe a rescue inhaler, in case you ever have that strong a reaction again. If you do, call me and come in for another exam. If it's severe go to the emergency room. Severe allergies can become life threatening under the right circumstances."

"How come I've never had a problem before?"

"It's possible that until now you've only had very light exposure, if any. It's also possible that you did have a reaction but just put it down to hay fever or a cold or something of that nature."

"I guess I just thought if I had a severe allergy it would have been more obvious years ago."

"It's also possible the allergy is a newer one or that it has increased in severity over time."

Cindy couldn't think of anything else to say. It didn't entirely make sense to her that all the symptoms she had experienced were the result of a tree allergy. What else could she say to the doctor, though? It wasn't like he could do a skin test to see if she was allergic to evil plain and simple.

"Thank you."

"You're welcome. You can go ahead and take an over-the-counter antihistamine for relief if minor symptoms spring up."

Half an hour later Cindy was back at work after dropping off her prescription at the pharmacy. She was just outside the office when she heard someone shout her name. She turned and saw Wildman running toward her, holding his hands out in front of him in an awkward manner.

"I need help," he called.

"With what?"

He didn't answer, but a moment later he was close enough that she could see why he was holding his hands out in front of him.

They were covered in blood.

6

"What happened?" Cindy asked, horrified.

"There was an explosion," Wildman said in distress.

"What! Where?"

"In the gym. One of the tubs of fake blood burst open and the stuff is everywhere."

Cindy sagged against the door in relief. "Fake blood."

"Yeah." He glanced down at his hands then back at her. "Oh gosh, you didn't think this was real blood did you?"

"It looks like real blood," she admitted.

He stared at her for a moment and then grinned and said, "Yes!" He punched the air with his fist and fake blood splattered on the door. "Oops."

"Let's get this cleaned up before this whole place looks like a massacre zone."

"Good idea," he said.

"Why don't you go wash off your hands in the bathroom and I'll meet you back in the gym with some cleaner and paper towels."

"Solid plan. I'm on it," he said, turning and heading for the nearest bathroom.

Cindy went into the office, deposited her purse in her desk drawer and waved at Geanie before heading for the supply closet. Armed with cleaning supplies she left and headed over to the gym.

She hadn't been inside since construction on the haunted house had started the week before. Temporary walls draped in black fabric had been put up in the left half of the building. More stacks of wood, ladders, tools, and boxes of props littered the right side. It was easy to see where the accident had occurred. There was a bright red spot in the middle of the chaos with streaks of red radiating out from it for several feet. Some had even splashed on the walls. As her eyes drifted upward she discovered that some of it had even managed to make it onto the ceiling.

A few seconds later Wildman came in and moved to stand beside her. "What do you think?" he asked.

"We're going to need a bigger ladder," she said.

"I should probably get the janitor," he said sheepishly.

Carl the janitor was prone to fits when things got too messy. Cindy wrinkled her nose at the thought of what he'd say about this place. Then again, even if it hadn't been a total mess he'd probably complain. He'd been the only person on staff to speak out against the haunted house complaining it would cause too much mess and would inspire hooligans to acts of vandalism.

Cindy took a deep breath. "No, we can handle this."

"Really?" Dave asked, the relief on his face nearly comical.

"Sure. We've dealt with worse."

That was true, but she still had no idea how they were going to reach the ceiling. She moved one of the trash cans in the room over closer to where they'd be working then tossed him one of the rolls of paper towels.

Before she started using the cleaner she began to mop up as much of the liquid as she could. Dave did the same.

"So, what all is going to be in the haunted house?" she asked as they worked.

"It's going to be awesome. The kids and I worked hard to pick some of the more frightening passages from the Bible, or at least ones that could easily be made frightening. We're starting off with the plagues in Egypt. We're going to show locusts consuming a body, have fake animal bodies representing the killing of the firstborn. The people in that sequence will be made up as dead, too, but they'll be the actual people instead of props so they can jump up and scare everyone who's going by."

"Are you using all this fake blood for the plague sequence?"

"Some of it. We're actually setting up a sort of sprinkler system so it looks like the walls are bleeding and we'll have buckets filled with the stuff."

"Gross, but cool."

"Thank you. Next we move on to the fiery furnace and we'll be blowing hot air through that section so people feel like they are Shadrach, Meshach, and Abednego. All around them we'll have people who are burning in the fire with skin melting off and everything."

"That is disgusting."

"I know! Isn't it awesome?"

It was something, alright. Just because it wasn't her cup of tea didn't mean that she was going to rain on his parade, especially not after he'd explained to her how important he thought this event was as far as outreach.

"What next?" she asked.

"We're going to show the battle where the Israelites under Barak defeated their enemies and the last part of it will show Sisera having the tent stake driven through his temple by Jael. One of our kids has an uncle who works for a special effects house in Los Angeles, and he's rigging up something for us so that it will look like she's actually hammering the stake into his skull and fake blood will spurt out. I can't wait to see that."

Cindy was very, very glad that she wouldn't be seeing that. Having mopped up a lot of the excess liquid she began to use some of the cleaner on part of the floor. "What next?" she asked.

"We're going to have one of those shaking floor sections and the scene is going to depict Samson pulling down the pillars of the building and slaying the Philistines. We have some fake rock falling effects to go in that section. So the ground will shake, it will look like the ceiling is collapsing. It's going to be epic."

"It sounds like it," she said. She had to admit to herself that she'd actually like to see that section because it sounded frightening without being gory.

"From there we move on to the New Testament and we have an assortment of demon possessed people roaming the maze trying to scare people. We also have a few squealing animatronic pigs to represent the herd that Jesus allowed the demons to go into when he cast them from the one man."

"That's going to be a bit disturbing. Not nightmare inducing at all," she said unable to hide the sarcasm in her voice.

"That's the point. Then we're going to show the slaughter of Christians in the coliseum but we'll make the people going through the maze feel like they're the ones being rounded up to be slaughtered. Then for the end we have a massive dragon with many heads."

"Ending with Revelation?"

"It's a classic."

"Sounds like this should be the most terrifying haunted house around."

"I really hope so. The kids are so excited and they've been working so hard. A lot of them have already got their friends and classmates to agree to come."

"You've done some amazing work," she told him.

"Thanks. There's still so much left to do, though. Opening night is in nine days."

It was hard to believe Halloween weekend was coming up that quickly. Time had flown since July. Before she knew it Christmas would be on them. She felt herself beginning to tense up at the thought of all the work ahead of her, but then forced herself to breathe and focus on the task at hand.

They worked on in silence for a couple more minutes. Finally they had the floor clean and they moved over to the wall.

"Can I ask you something?" Dave asked, his voice far more subdued and serious sounding.

"Sure," she said, wondering what was troubling him.

"Do you ever get bad feelings about things, like you know there's something wrong even if you can't quite place your finger on what it is?"

"I don't know, sometimes I guess. Although usually I have a pretty good idea what it is when I have that kind of feeling," she said. Her mind instantly conjured up images from the creepy house the day before. She wondered if Mark had found anything else about the case yet. She knew part of her would be unsettled until that one was solved. Part of her was also a little bit frightened to hear what that solution would be, though. She turned her attention back to the pastor. "Why do you ask?"

"It's just…I've had this weird feeling the last day or so and it keeps getting stronger. It's like my stomach is clenched in this tight little knot of anxiety and nothing I can do makes it better. I keep feeling like something bad, really bad, is about to happen. I don't know what, though, and as much as I'm trying to ignore it the feeling is getting worse. I'm really getting edgy and I don't like feeling this way."

"Have you ever felt this way before?" she asked.

He nodded. "I felt this way for three hours before I got the phone call that my father had been killed in a car crash."

"Sometimes with close relatives there can be an extra connection there, I guess," Cindy said. At least, she'd heard that could be the case although she didn't have family that she was close enough to that she'd have a connection like that with them.

"It's been other times, too. I had it the day we left for Green Pastures, but I ignored it, told myself I was crazy."

"Only you weren't," she said softly, fear rippling through her.

"I wasn't. I should have listened."

"You had no way of knowing what was going to happen or where or to whom. For all you knew it could have been something that was going to happen here or to a cousin halfway across the country."

"I know. That's what I tell myself when I start to freak out. This is the first time in a year-and-a-half that I've had that feeling, though. And I don't want to ignore it this time and assume that everything is going to be okay."

Cindy didn't know what to say, how to help him. "Have you prayed about it?"

"I was up half the night last night doing just that. Unfortunately I don't have any more clarity about what it could possibly be that's wrong."

She told herself that it was just the power of suggestion, or the memory of what she'd felt when she was in the basement the day before, but suddenly her stomach was also twisting in knots and she felt like she wanted to throw up. She said a quick prayer as she struggled to regain mastery over herself.

"Are you okay?" he asked suddenly.

"No, I'm a little freaked out to be honest," she told him.

"I'm sorry. I didn't mean to scare you. I just don't know what to do and I needed to talk to somebody about this. Somehow you seemed like the right person."

"I'm glad you could share with me. I just wish I knew what I could do to make you feel better or to stop whatever might be about to happen."

"Believe me, I understand," he said, sounding suddenly old and tired.

There was a loud crashing sound behind them and Cindy jerked around.

"What in tarnation is going on in here?" Carl bellowed, his voice echoing around the gym.

Cindy jumped and then faced him with a grimace. "We're just working on the haunted house."

"It looks like you're cleaning up a mess to me," he said, his voice only a notch below a shout.

"No messes here, just creation," she said defiantly. She wasn't in the mood for one of his temper tantrums.

She saw his eyes drift to the ceiling and she forced herself to stand her ground when he looked back at her.

"Make sure you clean it up then," he growled before turning and leaving the room.

"Thanks," Dave said, once the door had closed behind him.

"You're welcome. I figured neither of us really needed to deal with him today."

"You figured right. I know where he keeps the extra tall ladder. After he's left today I'll get it out and clean the ceiling."

"I think that might be a good idea," she agreed. "At least we've almost got the rest done."

"Thank you, for everything," he said.

"That's what friends are for," she said, forcing a smile onto her face. Inside, though, she was worrying about what he had told her about his feelings that something bad was going to happen. All she could do was pray that he was wrong.

When Mark had gotten into the office in the morning he'd discovered that they finally had an identification for the murdered girl. Her name was Cheyenne and she was seventeen, a high school senior who had been reported missing yesterday morning by her parents.

He went to see them and the visit made him sick to his stomach. He'd talked to lots of parents of victims before, just never when the victim was so young. He spent the entire time thinking about his own children and what he would be feeling if he was in their shoes and one of his children had been killed. It made it hard to stay on task and he silently cursed Liam for being on vacation.

In the end her parents had been no help at all. Their daughter was a nice girl, homeschooled, no close friends. At least, not any that they knew about. Then again, sometimes parents were the last to know what was really going on with their kids. Again he found himself worrying about his own children even though they were just babies.

When he'd finally finished talking with them he had no new leads to follow. He checked with the coroner but there was nothing new on that end either. The man was still running tests, taking samples.

Waiting was the part of the job that Mark hated the most. He did manage to swing by and pick up the crime scene photos he'd asked for duplicates of so that he could get Jeremiah's help with translation. Once he'd done that, he called the rabbi.

"Free for an afternoon meeting?" Mark asked.

"About the symbols?"

"Yes."

"I can be available at four."

"Perfect." It wasn't. He was antsy and wanted to do something now. He realized, though, that this would give him an opportunity to at least follow up on a few leads about Lizzie. "Any chance you can meet me at the park downtown? I'll be there checking a few things out."

"Okay."

Mark hung up and headed for the park. Michelle had mentioned that the coven met there near the big Redwood tree. He had checked and the full moon had been two nights before. It was a full moon the night the girl was killed, sacrificed, or whatever it had been. The very thought made him sick inside.

He was only about fifteen minutes away from the park and he made his way there, trying to keep his mind from playing worst case scenarios over and over again. That wasn't doing anyone any good, least of all him.

Once he had parked downtown he got out and strolled into the park. He could see half a dozen joggers from where he was walking. It was not the most secure or isolated location to hold a coven meeting, but then again the place was a lot more empty at night.

He made his way over to the Redwood tree and circled it slowly. He had no idea what he was looking for; he just hoped he'd know it when he saw it. After a minute he crouched down to get a better look at the dirt. He found a bit of candle wax. He kept going and a couple of feet away found a bit more. He kept moving until he had traced a rough circle connected by bits of candle wax. There were twelve piles of it and he wondered if that meant there had been twelve people present or if that was just the number of candles that had been set out to mark the circle.

He needed to find someone in the coven who would talk to him about Lizzie. He hadn't given up hope that she was safe and sound somewhere, oblivious to the fact that there were people worried about her.

He continued to inspect the area, but found nothing else of interest. He finally gave up and realized he was starving because he had missed lunch. Jeremiah would be there shortly, though, so he'd have to wait a few more minutes.

He sat down on a bench and tried to still his mind. He felt like it had been racing since he'd first seen Cheyenne's body in the basement yesterday. A couple minutes later he heard someone walk up beside him and he looked up.

"You have the pictures?" Jeremiah asked without preamble.

"Hello to you, too," Mark said. He handed him the envelope and he was grateful that the rabbi didn't open it right away. He wasn't in the mood to see the images again, especially not at that moment.

His phone pinged and he pulled it out. Traci had sent a text.

Found a perfect Breathless dress for you.

He shook his head as though she could see him and texted back. *You mean for you.* He put his phone away and stood up as his stomach growled.

"Everything okay?" Jeremiah asked.

"Yeah, Traci and I have just been having a discussion about what costumes we're wearing to Joseph and Geanie's party. What are you going as?"

"I don't know."

"You could go as a bullfrog."

"What?" Jeremiah said, gazing at him like he'd gone insane.

"Because of the song. You know, Jeremiah...bullfrog? Joy to the World?"

"You know that's not even my real name, right?"

"Forget it," Mark said, rolling his eyes. "You're not even any fun to tease these days."

He turned to go, but Jeremiah put a hand on his shoulder.

Mark turned.

"I'm...sorry," Jeremiah said as though it was torture to get the words out.

"Don't hurt yourself," Mark said sarcastically.

On the street a car backfired. Jeremiah dropped into a crouch and turned, his hand going to the back of his waistband. Just for a split second Mark saw the flash of metal before Jeremiah moved his hand and stood up.

7

"You're packing, aren't you?" Mark asked, unable to hide the shock in his voice.

Jeremiah turned and gave him a steely look, but said nothing.

Mark took a step closer and dropped his voice. "Why are you carrying a gun?"

"It's a dangerous world, Detective."

Mark wanted to hit him. He hated that Jeremiah more often than not called him Detective ever since he'd been back from Israel. It put artificial distance between them. It made him feel like they were strangers instead of friends.

"You listen to me. You are not okay. What happened over there messed you up good. Now you need to talk about it."

The corner of Jeremiah's mouth quirked up. "You want to counsel me?"

"I know, I wasn't easy on you when you needed to counsel me so I could go back on active duty on the force after I tortured that guy. But you stuck with it, and you made me talk, and that was what I needed. And don't think that it hasn't been on my mind that when you told me you understood and would have done the same thing that you weren't just speaking as a rabbi or some normal guy, but that you were a freaking spy and that killing came easy to you. Don't think that didn't mess me up a bit, having something like that in common with you once I realized all that."

"I'm not like you, Detective. Talking won't help fix me."

"No? Well, guess what, not talking certainly isn't doing the trick so let's try it the other way for a while and just see. Okay?"

"Fine."

"Okay, I'm starved. Let's go get something to eat and talk things over."

Jeremiah didn't protest so Mark turned and headed out of the park. He was relieved and a little surprised when the other man followed. They crossed the street and walked into a pub that Mark knew. It had good food and lots of it.

They grabbed a table and Mark ordered a beer and a burger. Jeremiah just shook his head at the waitress.

"Are you sure you don't want anything to drink?" Mark asked.

"You don't want me to drink," Jeremiah said. "I lose control and someone's going to get hurt."

"You need to loosen up," Mark said. "I'm not saying get drunk, just find some way to de-stress a bit. What helps you relax?"

Jeremiah just stared at him stonily. He wasn't going to make this easy. Mark rolled his eyes. "Sports, games?" His eyes drifted to the dartboard on the wall. "A good game of darts?"

"Darts? You're asking me to play a game of darts?"

"Yes. I'm asking you to play a game of darts."

Mark got up, walked over to the dartboard, and retrieved the darts from it. He returned and placed them on the table. He threw three, getting reasonably close to the bullseye, then took his seat and looked at Jeremiah.

Jeremiah stood, picked up a dart and jiggled it up and down in his hand. "Balance is off," he commented.

"How can you tell?" Mark asked.

"Experience." Jeremiah flipped the dart around and raised his arm. He was holding the dart with the pointed end facing away from the target. Before Mark could comment the rabbi threw the dart hard. It twirled in midair then buried itself in the bullseye. In rapid succession he did the same with the other two before sitting back down.

"See, that was fun," Mark said, forcing a smile.

"I'm not much of a game player," Jeremiah said, glaring at him.

The waitress brought Mark's beer and he sipped it gratefully. More than wanting to actually drink he wanted a moment to think through what he was going to say next.

He set the glass down slowly. "We've had a strange relationship since the beginning, you and I. We've been through a lot together, and honestly, it's reached the point where I count you as one of my closest friends. I didn't always know everything about you, but I didn't need to. I knew your character, your heart, and I knew enough to know that what was behind you wasn't pretty. I know that all of that came back to bite you in the butt and you're struggling with how to find yourself again."

"Or lose myself," Jeremiah said so quietly that he barely heard him.

"Or let go of the old," Mark said, refusing to acknowledge that the man he had known for years was not the real Jeremiah. "What you're having is the classic Superman/Clark Kent problem."

"Excuse me?"

"Which one is the real person, is the costume the disguise or are the glasses the disguise?"

"They both are to some extent."

"True, but the thing is, it's not one or the other. Clark Kent is just as real and just as much a part of his personality as Superman is. It's just the milder, more regular citizen version. He's still fighting for truth and justice, he's just doing it in the same way that regular people can. He loves Lois and doesn't love her any less when he puts on the tights. You have a past. Fine. It's part of who you are. But the rabbi who cares about people and helps his community is the same man who fought for his country and did what he could to help that community. You're making the world a better place in both of your chosen professions. One's just a bit more normal than the other."

Jeremiah stared at him intently and Mark couldn't tell what the other man was thinking or if he'd even managed to reach him. Finally Jeremiah said softly, "I don't want to wear the tights and cape ever again, but I'm having a problem putting on the glasses."

"Because you know it means you have to be normal and conform a bit more to society and that can be hard and stifling sometimes. It can also be rewarding, too."

"How?"

"For one, you can have a real relationship with Cindy and start a family with her."

Jeremiah started at that and Mark knew he'd struck a nerve. He leaned in. "Look, I know you love her. I know that's the only reason you came back here after whatever went down overseas. But what you're doing, this whole standing apart thing, isn't helping you heal and it isn't showing her that you're the guy for her. If you want to get better, if you want to feel connected to this place and the people around you, the best way you can do that is take your relationship with her to the next level."

"I don't want to hurt her."

"*I* don't want you to hurt her. I mean, in my perfect world you guys get married and have kids and our kids marry your kids or Geanie and Joseph's kids, and we're all just one big happy family."

Jeremiah blinked, clearly shocked by what Mark had said. Mark had to admit he was a little surprised himself. He cleared his throat. Now was not the time to hold back, even if it was uncomfortable for both of them.

"Look, you might not know it, but you have people here who love you. I don't make friends easy, in case you haven't noticed. Yet, I think of you as a friend. Actually, that doesn't even cover it. Given all that we've been through, I think of you as a brother."

And that realization rocked Mark like nothing else had in a long time.

Jeremiah bowed his head and Mark sat, quiet, not sure where they went from there. He wasn't used to being open, vulnerable and he could only hope that by being willing to be that way now he was somehow helping the other man.

Without looking up Jeremiah began to speak. "My family...we saw them when we were over there. It was a mistake, a bad call on my part when we needed somewhere to hide."

Mark felt himself go very still. Jeremiah was telling him something important, he could feel it, tell it in the tone of the rabbi's voice, see it in the tenseness of his shoulders.

He felt himself starting to panic, wondering if he was going to be able to rise to whatever challenge Jeremiah informed him of, but then he told himself that all he had to do in that moment was keep breathing and truly listen. That was the greatest gift he could give Jeremiah. It was something his own father had never been able to do for him. It was something he had sworn he would do differently with his own family and he had just told Jeremiah that he was included in that family. Now was a tipping point for both of them.

Just breathe and listen.

"My uncle knew more or less what I used to do for a living. He had told the others, but they didn't understand why I had stayed away, refused to see that it was because I loved them too deeply to endanger them. They were angry and unkind. My sister and my parents worst of all, my brother to a lesser degree. My sister-in-law, whom I'd never actually met, did her best to make it a joyous reunion, but she failed."

Jeremiah paused and Mark felt the urge to say something, express sympathy, ask a question, anything to break the silence. Jeremiah's head was still bowed, though, and he knew in his gut that the story didn't end there.

Just listen.

This time it didn't even seem like him telling himself that, but some other voice that was gently urging him to be still, and a sense of peace that was different from anything he had ever experienced filled him at that moment.

"Cindy was with me. I wanted to protect her. We had used a cover when we reached the country, something that would ensure that we could stay together through all the craziness that was happening. I knew for all our sakes that I had to maintain that cover."

Jeremiah paused again, and Mark found himself leaning forward. Knowing the other man as he did, having been through some of the things they had been through, he was pretty sure he knew what that cover had been. He didn't ask, though, didn't prompt. He just...listened.

"I introduced Cindy to my mother, father, uncle, siblings and their spouses as my wife. My uncle and my sister-in-law welcomed her with open arms, no questions asked."

Jeremiah struggled to a halt again. His shoulders were hunched now and pain had crept into his voice. It took everything Mark had in him not to say a word, knowing that he had to just let Jeremiah get the story out in his own time. He glanced up just in time to see the waitress heading his way with his burger. He made eye contact with her and shook his head.

Miraculously she seemed to understand. She nodded and headed back to the kitchen. His stomach rumbled angrily, but he knew that if she had interrupted that Jeremiah would have shut down and never finished telling the story. And clearly telling the story was what he needed to do to start getting over what had happened overseas.

Mark had known there had been violence, bloodshed, terrorists, and danger to both Cindy and Jeremiah. He had assumed that all of that, coupled with having to be that man again, part of that world again, was what had caused him to shut down and be so distant. Mark realized now, though, that even if that was what Jeremiah believed, the problem was actually far more personal.

"The others...they were cruel. They were angry that I had married outside my faith. They lashed out at Cindy. And do you know what she did? She defended me, us, our relationship even though it wasn't real. And I knew then that even though we weren't married that she meant far more to me than anyone else in that room and that I couldn't tolerate them not accepting her. The things she said...I wanted to cry...and given how beautiful, how eloquent, the fact that the others weren't moved shocked me. Suddenly everything was so clear. The family I had tried so hard to protect didn't deserve my protection. But Cindy did. She deserved all the love and loyalty I could ever show her."

Jeremiah's voice had started to shake and Mark's heart ached for him even as he pictured the scene and how terrible it must have been. Jeremiah was the strongest person he knew and to see him hurt, vulnerable, was frightening and told him so much about what that reunion had cost him.

"I realized that if they couldn't accept her, then they could never be part of my life again, not even for a moment. And for once it had nothing to do with me trying to protect them. It was all about me protecting Cindy. I tore my clothes for my parents, my sister and her husband. I let them know that they were dead to me and I to them and that we would never see each other again. For the sake of my sweet, compassionate sister-in-law who embraced Cindy and called her sister I did not rend my clothes for my brother or her. Nor did I rend them for my uncle. Still, it is unlikely that I will meet any of those three again in this life. I chose my family. I chose Cindy. And God help me, I think she chose me. And I feel guilt and shame every day

74

because she deserves better than me, but I can't find the strength to let her go."

Jeremiah looked up and Mark was stunned to see tears running down his cheeks. He had never thought he would see the other man cry. He was at a loss as to what to do.

Speak.

The voice that wasn't his came again, prompting him. He reached across the table and gripped Jeremiah's arm. "You need to stop focusing on yourself and start focusing on her. You say she chose you. Then she did so of her own free will, knowing who you are and who you were and everything you can be. If you love her then you need to let her make her own decision in this matter, not try to control it for her."

"What are you saying?" Jeremiah asked.

"I'm saying that you're going about this all wrong. What you realized when dealing with your family was true. Cindy is more family to you than they are. So, instead of trying to find the strength to let her go, you need to love her enough to find the strength to hold on tight to her and let her love make you the man you want to be. You know what happened to me. You know that Traci has been my salvation. She has been the lifeline I have clung to. She has made me a better man because I strive to be for her sake. You must let Cindy do the same for you."

"There are obstacles in our way."

"And when did obstacles ever stop you? Look, I never believed there was any kind of higher power before I met you two. But working with you, getting to know you, watching the way things have gone in your life, even I've begun to believe that maybe there is a God out there. And if there is only one thing I'm sure I know about Him it's that He seems to want the two of you together. The more you fight that, the more miserable it makes you."

"And what if she wakes up one day and realizes she made a mistake?" Jeremiah asked, fear in his voice.

"Then by God you fight for her with everything you have in you, and if there's one thing I know you know how to do it's fight."

The corner of Jeremiah's mouth turned up slightly. "You have no idea just how well I can fight."

"Then stop fighting against Cindy and start fighting for Cindy."

"I think it's a bit more than that," Jeremiah said.

Mark cocked his head to the side. "How do you figure?"

Jeremiah leaned back slightly. "When I came to California something struck me about the people here that was different than anywhere I'd ever been before."

"I can think of a number of ways that could be true. After all, we are the land of the fruits, the nuts, and the flakes so they say."

Jeremiah actually gave him a full smile for that one. "That aside, what struck me was that blood family is less important here than anywhere else I've ever been. People here choose the people they want in their lives and they make friends their family. Look at Cindy. She has parents and a brother and yet they're not the ones she considers close to her."

Mark nodded. "There's a saying here. You can't choose your relatives, but you can choose your family."

"I never understood that. In Israel, in my brother's house, I had my first moment of enlightenment about that and how it comes to be. But I can honestly say I didn't truly understand it until you told me I was like your brother."

Mark nodded, not trusting himself to speak in that moment.

"My first thought was that I had a brother and he and I aren't close so it seemed somewhat absurd to me. Then, I realized that you truly have been more of a brother to me than my own. You have been there for me, you have fought and bled and broken oaths and laws for me. And when things were bad, when I knew I was being recalled in July, you were the one I turned to. I had spent so much time being wary of you, afraid to be myself around you because I was afraid you'd figure out who I had been in my past, or, at least, *what* I had been. Yet, when everything went wrong and fell apart, you were the one I turned to because you were the one I trusted to understand and to help. You were able to do for me what my own flesh and blood couldn't. And when I came back broken, distant, you fought to stay close and to be a part of my life. That's something my family wasn't capable of."

Mark was struggling not to cry. He had definitely grown up in one of those households where it wasn't seen as manly. It was hard, though, because Jeremiah's words touched him. He'd been telling the truth. Making friends wasn't easy for him. He walked around encased in a protective, sarcastic shell that very few had ever cracked.

He cleared his throat. "If we were in the second grade this would be the part where we'd cut our palms, shake hands and declare ourselves blood brothers."

"I think there's already been enough blood spilled between us," Jeremiah said.

"Agreed." Mark stretched out his hand. Jeremiah took it and they shook solemnly.

"Brothers," Mark said.

"Brothers," Jeremiah affirmed.

"Now, as your brother I think I need to tell you to go make nice with Cindy or I'll be obliged to kick your ass."

Jeremiah laughed out loud and the sound clearly surprised him as much as it did Mark. "It would be amusing to watch you try."

"Well, just as a warning, I don't fight fair," Mark said.

"And I don't even comprehend the meaning of that," Jeremiah countered.

Mark saw the waitress over Jeremiah's shoulder. She looked at him and he nodded. A few seconds later she brought over his burger. It tasted like it had been sitting under a heat lamp the entire time, but it was worth it because he felt like they had made a breakthrough. Jeremiah might still have a lot of crap to work through, but at least he was on the road to being his old self.

"Sure you don't want something to eat?" he asked after his third bite.

Jeremiah shook his head. "No. I figure I need to go talk to Cindy, get a few things straightened out."

"Smart move."

Jeremiah stood. "Thank you...Mark."

"You're very welcome."

"And for what it's worth, I was wrong. Clearly I did need to talk."

"Nailed it," Mark said before taking another bite.

Jeremiah turned and left the bar. After he had gone the waitress came over. "Everything okay?" she asked.

Mark nodded. "Just had to work some stuff out with my brother," he said before he could stop himself.

She nodded and wandered off, leaving Mark alone with his thoughts. *Clearly fatherhood has made me all kinds of sentimental*, he reflected. *Maybe Traci's not the only one having crazy hormone fluctuations.* But, having lived without that kind of sentiment for much of his life, he was pretty sure this was a good thing. At least whatever mistakes he made with his family would be his and not someone else's.

He had just finished his meal and was paying when his phone rang. A minute later he was up and heading for the door. Just when he was reflecting on brotherly love and getting ready to do something ridiculous like break into a chorus of kumbaya he was brought crashing back to the real world by being sent out to a crime scene. Someone had been murdered. The sad truth was that about fifteen percent of people murdered were murdered by a spouse or close family member. It helped put the whole brotherly love thing in perspective.

The location of the body was on a little league baseball field of all places. Apparently it had been discovered and called in by the groundskeeper. More than that Mark didn't know, but he wished they'd called in someone else. He already had his hands full.

When he arrived on the scene there were already three patrol cars there and officers were busy cordoning off the area. Sitting on one of the bottom benches in the stands was a man with graying hair who looked to be in his fifties. He was sitting with his head buried in his hands. Mark guessed that he was the groundskeeper who had called it in. He'd talk to him after he took a look at the body.

He walked out onto the field. A couple of officers were busy setting up some portable lights. He could see a dark shape lying on the ground halfway between the pitcher's mound and home plate and he felt a flicker of disgust. Was nothing sacred anymore?

He recognized a couple of officers from the day before who glanced at him then hurriedly glanced away. It struck him as odd and he wondered what was going on that they were acting so skittish.

A few moments later he was standing next to the body and he suddenly understood. He looked down and thought that he was going to be sick. A girl was staked out on a pentagram in an identical pose to the one Cheyenne had been in. She, too, was dead, her eyes locked wide in terror.

The only difference was this time it was someone he knew.

8

The dead girl was Lizzie's roommate, Michelle. Less than twenty-four hours ago she had been alive, talking to him in her apartment and now she was dead, murdered by some psychopath. But why? It couldn't be random. She had to have been chosen. It was too crazy to actually be a coincidence. Was it because of something she was into, or something Lizzie was involved with, or just because he had gone to see her and he was the detective investigating the first murder?

A chill danced up his spine. If it was because of him then no one he knew was safe. If it was because of Lizzie then Traci and the kids could still be in danger. He started to feel a little dizzy and he bent over, hands braced on his knees, and tried to get his head lower to increase the oxygen flow.

"You alright, Detective?"

He turned to see a woman in a black suit standing behind him. She had a sleek blond ponytail and piercing eyes.

"Who are you?" he asked.

"Trina Mills, F.B.I.." She pulled out her badge and showed it to him.

"What is the F.B.I. doing here?" he asked, startled.

"We caught wind of this case earlier today. I hopped a plane and your boss was kind enough to tell me where I could find you. I see I'm just in time for the party."

"That's how you got here, but it still doesn't answer why," he said.

"Let's just say that some of the details of this case match up with others I've investigated."

"Serial killer," Mark said, feeling his chest tighten even more. That was the last thing they needed. The town had barely recovered from its last serial killer.

"Perhaps, but let's just say there is a greater pattern, a greater concern."

There was something she clearly didn't want to tell him. That was not particularly surprising. In his experience the F.B.I. usually kept their cards close to their vest.

He forced himself to straighten slowly as the dizziness finally faded away. "You didn't answer my question," she said. "Are you okay?"

"Not really. This girl was my sister-in-law's roommate. And I was talking to her last night about her concerns that my sister-in-law hadn't been home in a week and she had a bad feeling something had happened to her."

Trina whistled. "Well that puts you smack dab in the middle of this mess, especially when you consider that you're the detective assigned to the first pentagram murder."

"Don't I know it," he said with a grunt. "And please, let's not call them the pentagram murders. That's just the sort of name the press loves to get wind of and run with making all our jobs so much harder."

"It's your turf, I've no desire to make things harder on you," Trina said with a shrug.

There was something about her that was slightly off. He totally believed that she was a Fed. She had that vibe to her, but there was something else. Before he could stop himself he asked her bluntly, "So, are you with the unit that investigates occult crimes?"

"Among other things," she said.

He blinked in surprise, shocked that she hadn't bothered to deny it. He decided to press his luck further. "You ever seen some of these symbols that she's got written all over her?"

"A few," Trina admitted. "Though certainly not all of them."

"Care to share?"

She pointed to a marking on the girl's left hand. "That one is an ancient symbol representing immortality."

"Not that it did Michelle any good," he said morbidly. Truth be told he was struggling to keep it together and not let worry for Traci or her sister overtake him completely. The more he stared at Michelle's body the harder that was getting.

"Tell you what, you take a look around, and I'll do the same. Then we'll question the man who found the body together. After that we'll have a sitdown and you can fill me in on everything I need to know."

"You're the boss," he said.

"Think of me more as a willing partner with a bigger computer database and a lot more experience with...this type...of case."

And there was something about the way she said those last few words that made him wish he'd never encountered this type of case, whatever it was.

The crime scene reminded him of the last one. The location was completely different, but everything else was the same, right down to the markings on the body and the fact that both women had been wearing similar white nightgowns. He told Trina that. She had nodded and taken it all in. The groundskeeper had no information to share other than that he'd been there to check on a couple of things, saw her, and called the police.

"So, what did you see?" he finally asked Trina as they were standing out by his car.

"Pretty much what you did. I'll be interested to know what the coroner finds, for both bodies."

"You and me both."

She shook her head. "Look, I'm jetlagged, you look tired, let's regroup in the morning, okay?"

"That works for me."

She nodded, then headed for her car. Once there she turned and looked at him. "Detective, it's a nice clear night, the moon is bright. Good night for a coven meeting, don't you think?"

Before he could say anything she got in the car and drove off, but she had given him an idea. He pulled out his phone and called Liam. To his surprise his partner picked up.

"Why are you answering your phone, you're on vacation," he growled.

"Why are you calling me when you know I'm on vacation?" Liam countered.

Mark sighed. "Because I need your help with something. It's so potentially dangerous that even I'm not stupid enough to go it alone."

"That's saying something," Liam said.

"Yeah. So, where did you end up going?"

"I'm home right now. Just been doing a lot of day trips, doing all the touristy things I've never done. Did an overnight trip to San Francisco, but that's the farthest away I've gone."

"I hate to ask, but-"

"I can be dressed in five minutes. Where do you want me to meet you?"

"The park downtown. Meet me in the parking area on the south side."

"Done."

Liam hung up and Mark got into his car. He hoped that Trina was right and that it was a good night for a coven meeting because he had questions and he hoped some wiccan somewhere had answers. Before he could find out, though, he had to make sure Traci was okay.

Cindy had made it through the rest of the day and as soon as she got home she changed into her fluffiest, fuzziest fleece pajamas which sported cavorting cats. She was standing in front of the refrigerator unenthusiastically taking inventory of her leftover options when the doorbell rang.

She closed the refrigerator and headed to the front door debating whether it was a get out the vote volunteer or Jehovah's Witnesses at the door. She'd had visits from both groups a lot lately. When she looked through the peephole, though, she was surprised to see Jeremiah standing there with a large bag in his arms.

She opened the door and stepped back to let him enter. She closed the door and followed him into the kitchen where he set the bag down on the counter.

"I brought Chinese food. I hope that's alright," he said.

"Sure," she said, struggling to make sense of his sudden appearance. "Did we have plans tonight?" she asked, searching her memory and not coming up with anything.

"No, we didn't," he said. He cleared his throat slightly and turned to her. "But I thought we needed to talk."

She felt a slight sinking sensation in her stomach. She'd been wanting to have a real conversation with him for weeks and this should be a good thing, but the way he phrased it made her nervous.

"About what?" she asked cautiously.

"About everything that happened in Israel. About...us."

She still couldn't judge what type of conversation it was going to be because he had his head down a bit and wasn't making eye contact with her. It certainly wasn't looking good, she thought.

"I'm sorry I've been so distant. I've been struggling with a lot of things."

"I know," she said softly. "And I want to help you with those."

"The truth is, I haven't wanted help. I'm not sure if I truly didn't think anyone could help or I was just afraid to open up."

She stepped forward and put her hand on his chest. "Whatever you need, I'm here for you," she said, trying to meet his eyes.

She finally succeeded, and his eyes were burning with intensity. The look in his eyes reminded her of those few stolen moments on the Temple Mount after they had defeated the terrorists and her heart began to beat faster at the memory.

"I know, you've been a saint. The problem is, I haven't been here for you. Everything that happened, it can't have been easy on you and I wasn't here for you to talk to. That was wrong, and I'm sorry. Can you forgive me?"

Something had changed since she'd seen him the night before. She had no idea what, but she was beginning to feel a profound sense of relief. She stepped closer to him and put her other hand on his chest as well. "I can forgive you," she said, gazing up into his eyes. "But on one condition."

She was playing with fire and she knew it, but weeks of uncertainty and growing frustration could not be undone with mere words at this point.

"What is it?" he asked, sounding worried.

It was now or never. She suddenly wished she was wearing something less fleecy and more attractive. There was no help for it, though, and she had already committed herself.

"I need you to prove to me that the things you said that day weren't just in the heat of the moment, that you meant them then, and that you still do."

She started to slide her arms up to his neck. His phone rang and he stepped back and pulled it out of his pocket. She felt like screaming, but she forced herself to take several deep breaths.

"It's Mark," Jeremiah told her. He wasn't sure if the detective had perfect timing or terrible timing. He knew that Cindy had wanted him to kiss her, but there was so much he wanted to talk over with her first. He answered the phone. "Hello?"

"Did you make nice with Cindy?"

"Yes."

"Give her some reassurance?"

"I tried."

"Good, because the three of us have got to get our mojo back in a serious way."

"What's going on?" Jeremiah asked, hearing the anxiety in Mark's voice.

"There's been another murder, same kind of thing. Only this time it was my sister-in-law's roommate. Worse, she was just telling me last night that Lizzie hasn't been home for a week and she ran up the red flag and called Amber who called Traci who sent me over there to investigate."

Jeremiah turned to look at Cindy and put the phone against his chest to muffle his voice from Mark. "Traci's sister Lizzie is missing and her roommate who alerted the family just turned up dead, the second victim of whoever killed the girl in the basement."

Cindy went pale, but nodded resolutely. "We've got to get over there." She walked over to the counter, picked up her purse, and started for the door.

"Um, maybe you want to put some clothes on if you intend to solve mysteries tonight," he said.

She glanced down at her pajamas and blushed. "Right, on it." She put down her purse and headed for her bedroom.

Jeremiah put the phone up to his ear. "I'm back."

"Put some clothes on? Just exactly *how* did you make nice with Cindy?" Mark asked.

Jeremiah was about to snap at him that it was none of his business, but he remembered their earlier conversation and thought about what Cindy would want him to say. "I came over just a couple of minutes ago to surprise her with dinner, and she was already in her pajamas. Which she is still wearing," he said, just to make things crystal clear.

Although as soon as he said that he imagined her in her room right then taking them off in order to change into other clothes. The thought was distracting to say the least and he actually missed whatever it was Mark had said next. It was probably just as well.

"Where do you want us to meet you?" Jeremiah asked.

"Better make it our house. Traci's going to want to be a part of this given that it's her sister we're talking about."

"Okay, we can be there in fifteen."

"Actually, get started without me. I've got a couple leads I have to chase down first. I know she's going to want to talk and the sooner you guys are over there watching out for her and the babies, the more settled I'll feel."

"You think they're in danger?" he asked sharply.

"I don't know what to think at this point. Look, I've got to run. I'll be there as soon as I can."

Mark hung up and Jeremiah stood there for a moment trying to process everything. Then he walked forward and knocked on Cindy's door.

"Almost ready," she called.

"It sounds like we need to get over to Mark and Traci's as soon as possible," he said.

"Let's take the food over with us," Cindy suggested.

"Good idea. I got a little carried away with the ordering and there's more than enough to share," he said.

"Great."

She opened the door. She was wearing a green satin tank top and a black skirt. She was stunning. She brushed her hair back with a careless hand and he felt his pulse begin to race. She picked up a light sweater and put one arm into it.

"What do you think we'll be doing? Do you think I need to put something warmer on, like a heavier sweater? Or I could put on jeans. I mean, if we're going to be possibly out-"

Jeremiah reached out and pulled her to him. The feel of the satin beneath his fingers made his head spin as he kissed her. This was what she wanted, proof that he had meant everything he said. After a startled moment she began to kiss him back, twisting her fingers in his hair. If she knew how wild that drove him she wouldn't do it. He should tell her.

He broke off the kiss and his eyes took in the room behind her, and then he heard himself saying, "Actually I think you're a bit overdressed."

"It's what I wore to work today. You think the shirt is too fancy?" she asked.

"I don't think the clothes are too nice. I think you're wearing too many of them," he said, pulling the sweater she'd half put on off her and tossing it onto the floor before pulling her in tighter. He wrapped his arms around her, molding her body to his and all the careful control he'd built up, all the walls, came crashing down.

"You've been so cold, distant," she said when he began trailing kisses down her throat.

"I was wrong, so wrong. I'm sorry. I should never have let you doubt me, doubt what I feel." He buried his face in her hair and breathed in its scent.

"It's okay," she said, her voice shaking slightly. "Just don't do it again."

He nodded and just stood there for a moment, holding her. Finally he pulled away. His heart was still racing but he felt like he had regained mastery over himself. "We should get over to Traci and Mark's."

"Okay, but first I have one question."

"What is it?"

"I'm needing a little clarity on my outfit," she said with a smirk.

With a straight face he said, "Wear a sweater. Wear two sweaters. And jeans, too. The ugliest, most poorly fitted jeans you can find."

"So then I won't be attractive?"

He shook his head. "Don't count on it. I have a feeling you could wear burlap and it would still be sexy."

She blushed even as she laughed and the sound almost made him forget his promise to Mark, his concern for Traci, and the fact that her sister could be in serious trouble.

Almost, but not quite.

"We better get out of here," he said. And suddenly he felt an urgency about it, like there was somewhere they needed to be and fast.

Cindy frowned. "Is something wrong?"

He nodded. "Yes, I just wish I knew what it was."

9

Mark had a sick feeling in his stomach as he waited for Liam to join him at the park. He was way, way outside his comfort zone and had been since the first body had shown up on Monday. He tried to rehearse in his mind how he was going to approach the coven, but realized he had no idea what to expect. They could be hostile, angry at the intrusion by outsiders.

Then again they were holding their meeting in a public place, in the park in downtown Pine Springs. They couldn't be expecting complete privacy. For that there was forest not half an hour away. Then again since everything that had happened at Green Pastures a while back he wouldn't blame anyone for never wanting to go into the woods again, ever.

Maybe that was why they met in the park. It was safer. Also closer. By meeting late at night they also minimized the risk of interruption so just because they were in a public place didn't mean they were ready and willing to accept visitors.

He wondered why of all the spots in the park they gathered near the lone Redwood tree. He wondered if it had some mystical significance. When Lizzie first got into Wicca she'd talked about different plants symbolizing different things and being used in various rituals.

He sighed and leaned his head back for a moment. Maybe if they hadn't given her space, but had butted into her life earlier none of this would be happening now. Still, he didn't want to believe that the deaths were Lizzie's fault. And it wasn't just because he didn't want to be known as the cop that locked up his wife's sister.

Lizzie used to be a lot gentler when she was younger although she'd always been a bit moody. Sensitive, that's how Traci had once described her sister and it made sense.

Liam's car pulled up next to his and Mark got out. "Thanks for coming," he said as Liam came around to stand next to him a few seconds later.

"What are partners for?" Liam asked with a shrug.

"Did you at least see some interesting tourist places?" Mark asked, feeling the urge to talk to fill the silence, trying to calm his own jitters.

"Took the nighttime tour of Alcatraz when I went up to San Francisco."

"I bet that was disturbing."

"Made me glad I became a cop. When I was little my mother swore I could go either way."

"Not you," Mark said. "You're a straight and narrow type of guy and I'm sure you were the same way as a kid."

Liam just shrugged. "So, care to tell me what we're doing in the park late at night?"

"We're going to see some wiccans about a witch."

"Okay, you lost me."

"I'm not even sure I understand. We're going to interrupt a coven meeting, hopefully, to try and get some answers. Stick close."

"Just out of curiosity why is it that we always get the weird cases?" Liam asked.

"Just lucky I guess. You wouldn't want life to get boring, would you?"

"No, but every once in a while it might be nice, you know, as a novelty."

Mark shook his head and clicked on his flashlight. "Okay, let's go."

They had parked fairly close to where the giant Redwood tree was. He'd hoped that if they had the element of surprise on their side that even if coven members decided to run, they'd at least be able to catch one or two. Hopefully those would actually have information worth knowing.

"You want to fill me in on what's going on?" Liam asked.

"Later," Mark growled. "For now, maintain silence. We don't want to spook them."

Which is ironic, because I'm the one who's freaked out, he thought.

They made their way stealthily through the park. He kept the flashlight low, sweeping on the ground just in front of them so they could see where they were stepping and hopefully not trip over any inconvenient roots.

As they neared the tree he could hear voices. They were low and it was hard to make out what they were saying. He felt his heart begin to pound harder and his palms began to sweat. He didn't like the thought of bearding a coven in its den.

He saw pinpricks of light next, candles placed on the ground in a rough circle as he had suspected they might be. The coven was here, and the closer he got the more he hated this whole situation.

He slowed down and started walking even more softly. He wanted to get a good look at the circle before revealing their presence if he could. He counted a dozen people standing a shoulder's width apart from each other, just inside the circle drawn by the candles. All of them wore cloaks, half of them had the hoods drawn up to obscure their faces while the other half didn't. Apparently some of them didn't care who knew what they believed.

He and Liam were very close now although the others still seemed to be oblivious to their presence which was a good thing. He couldn't make out exactly what they were doing, but it was clear there was a lot of gesturing that went along with the words they were saying.

After another minute of that a woman stepped into the center of the circle and raised her arms. "Merrily met and merrily part. Blessed be."

"Blessed be," the others intoned. Then everyone reached down, picked up a candle and blew it out.

The moon was shining brightly enough that there was still enough light to see by. Everyone took off their cloak so maybe he'd been wrong about it being meant to obscure. Maybe it was just like a ceremonial dress. Whatever was going on it seemed like the formalities were over and now people just started chatting with each other. He overheard one of the women mention her daughter's piano recital the next afternoon while two men were talking about getting the transmission fixed on one of their cars.

And suddenly Mark felt himself relaxing. Without their cloaks and candles they seemed more like regular people. He suddenly found it hard to believe that the people he heard chatting so casually about the same kinds of things other people did could be behind such brutal sacrifices.

Throwing caution to the wind he stepped forward. The woman who had been in the center of the circle noticed him first. She looked at him with curiosity and walked forward. Two things struck him about her right away. The first was just how curly her red hair was and the second was that she was wearing what looked like a hand-knitted sweater.

He blinked in surprise and wondered if this was Sweater Girl that Lizzie used to talk about with her roommate.

"Can I help you?" she asked.

"Yes, are you the one in charge here?"

"Tonight I am," she said. "We often take turns."

"So, you're not like the high priestess?"

"No, our coven is run a little more democratically than some of the more traditional ones," she said.

He pulled out his badge and her look of curiosity turned to one of concern. "My name is Detective Mark Walters and this is my partner. I was wondering if I could ask you about one of your covenmates, I guess you would call her."

"Who?"

"A girl named Lizzie Matthews."

"Lizzie, yes, I know her, but she's not one of our covenates, not anymore."

"When did she leave?"

"It was quite a while ago. I'd say about two years."

"Can you tell me why?"

The woman's face changed subtly and her eyes became more guarded. "Can I ask what this is about?"

"She was reported missing about a week ago and a few hours ago her roommate was found, murdered."

"Oh my!" Sweater Girl said, her hand flying to her mouth. "That's terrible!"

"Yes, and we're eager to figure out what's going on and to find Lizzie. She might be in terrible danger."

"Of course, I'll do anything I can." She turned and called out, "Albert, can you come here a moment?"

A large, sweaty bald man walked over, his face jovial and grinning from ear-to-ear. "Do we have newcomers Matilda?" he asked.

"No, Albert. These are the police. Lizzie Matthews has gone missing and she may be in danger. I'm going to talk to them for a while. Can you ask the others if any of them has heard from her recently or might know anything about her whereabouts?"

"Of course," he said, the grin quickly disappearing from his face. Matilda led Mark and Liam away as Albert began to speak to the others. Once they were out of easy earshot she faced them.

"When Lizzie joined our coven she was very eager to learn, excited about everything. She'd had no real exposure to religion of any kind growing up."

Mark nodded, but didn't say anything. He was going to avoid mentioning his connection to Lizzie if he could. The less Matilda knew about him, Lizzie, and everything that was going on the better for all of them.

"She took to it quickly, learned as much as she could, but after a couple of months I could tell that something was wrong."

"What?"

"She wasn't as happy as she had once been. In fact she was getting more sullen, withdrawn. I suspected something might be upsetting her in her personal life, but she wouldn't talk about it. Then she began questioning some of our most basic teachings. I could tell that she was no longer satisfied with our way of worship or the things that she was learning. She started asking a lot of questions of more established members, questions that had to do with the study of dark magic. She was making some people uncomfortable. She was becoming obsessed with power, how to achieve it, how to keep it, that sort of thing."

"And what did you tell her?"

"That she was focused on the wrong things. I told her Wicca was about being a part of something and not dominating something."

"Do you have any idea what she might have been after?"

"Power, that is my only guess. If it was something more specific than that, I wasn't privy to it. It had reached the point where we knew we were going to have to ask her to leave, which broke my heart. We try so very hard to be inclusive that it is a tragedy when we have to instead exclude. However, it seemed that she had tired of us long before we had tired of her. She quit the coven, said she'd found a better one, a coven that was more suited to her needs. We let her go with our blessings and a heavy heart."

"And you haven't seen her since?"

"I don't believe so," Matilda said.

"Any idea about who this other coven was she had joined or where they'd meet?"

"Not really, but two of our other members left at the same time she did and I figure they went on together."

"Who was this?" Mark asked sharply.

"Peter and Vanessa. They were also drawn more to the darker side of things."

"Do you have contact information for either of them?"

"I'm afraid not. I lost my phone while I was on vacation last year and with it all my old contacts. I'm usually the one who sends out reminders about meetings and things so I had everyone's numbers. It's possible someone else knows how to contact them. I can ask."

"That would be greatly appreciated."

"Consider it done. Is there anything else I can help with?"

"Not that I can think of at the moment, but I'm going to leave you with my card and I'd appreciate it if I could get your contact information."

"Of course."

She gave him her number and he wrote it down in his notepad before handing her one of his cards. She tucked it into the pocket of her jeans. "Detective, there is actually something you might be able to help me with, if you don't mind."

"What's that?" he asked, somewhat surprised. Most people being questioned by a police officer, even if they were innocent, were still eager to see the officer go.

"Something weird has happened. I have a black cat."

Mark couldn't stop himself from smirking.

She rolled her eyes at him in response. "I know, very cliché. Look, black cats are the least likely to be adopted and the most likely to be put down. I happen to be a cat person and I'm a sucker for underdogs. Well, my cat went missing a couple of nights ago."

"I'm more of a dog person myself, but isn't that kind of normal for cats to come and go sometimes?" Mark asked.

"Some cats, sure, but not mine. I don't let her run around outside because I don't want her to get hurt or killed by a car or another animal or anything. I have a screened in porch she likes to hang out in. Two nights ago I got home and I couldn't find her. I looked everywhere. Then I noticed that there was a tear in the screen in the patio. It was just big enough for her to get through. The thing is, there wasn't a tear in that screen when I left in the morning."

"Maybe she saw something on the outside she wanted, a bird or lizard maybe and clawed her way out."

"Ordinarily I'd think so, too. She was a rescue, though, and when I got her the previous owners had her front paws declawed. That type of damage would have been impossible for her to cause."

"That is odd," Mark said with a frown. "Maybe she had a boyfriend, another cat who came by and sprung her loose?"

"The only other cat on our block belongs to the little old lady across the street. When I went over to ask her if she'd seen Ebony she told me that she hadn't and that her own cat Whiskers had gone missing the day before. Her cat, by the way, is also black."

"Is she also a-"

"Born again Christian, so no, she's not a Wiccan, if that's what you were about to ask."

"I was going to say conscientious cat owner," Mark fibbed.

"Yes. Her cat does occasionally sneak out the back door, but he never goes far and he's always back for dinner. We've called all the shelters, put up flyers, and there's no sign of our cats."

"That's tragic, but I don't see how you think I can help," Mark said.

Matilda glanced around then stepped in closer. "My cousin works for the police department. He told me that there was an occult murder, human sacrifice."

Mark barely managed to keep himself from swearing. He did manage to keep his face neutral neither denying nor admitting anything.

"Obviously I'm hoping it's not true, and that whatever's going on you catch the sick monster behind it. But it's got me worried. A lot of shelters don't adopt out black cats during the month of October."

"Because they're afraid that once the Halloween party is over people will dump their black cats right back at the shelter?"

She shook her head. "That's not the worst of it. There are some sick people in this world, people who do things like what happened to that girl. Black cats get hurt a lot at this time of the year. I can't stand the thought that someone might do something to Ebony and Whiskers. So, please, catch these people and tell the other officers to be on the lookout for black cats."

"I will," he promised.

"Thank you. I'll call you in the morning with whatever information I can get."

"Good. I'll talk to you then," Mark said.

He turned and he and Liam made their way swiftly back to their cars. Once there Mark leaned against his, trying to regain his composure.

"So, what are you going to want me to help with?" Liam asked.

'Maybe nothing. Maybe everything. Go, enjoy the rest of your vacation, but do me a favor and stay close to your phone."

"Will do," Liam promised before driving off.

Mark got into his own car. It was past time he made it home to Traci. He just wished he had something new to tell her about the whereabouts of her sister.

Cindy, Jeremiah, and Traci were sitting around Traci's kitchen table drinking orange juice. As Cindy poured herself another glass she reflected that at least Traci seemed much calmer than when they had first arrived. It had also been kind of fun to help her put the babies to bed. She still couldn't believe how fast the twins were growing.

After that they had been discussing the case and how it could pertain to Lizzie while they waited for Mark to come home. Well, that, and there was some brief discussion of the upcoming costume party. Cindy was disgusted that Jeremiah still was not on board with the whole couples costume thing.

"Wasn't your grandmother's sister a Wiccan?" Jeremiah asked Cindy out of the blue.

"She was. How did you know that?"

"You told me about the Easter you spent at her house when we were swapping worst holiday meal stories."

"Oh, that's right," Cindy said with a grin. "The ham my dad kept stabbing with her ceremonial knife while my brother was screaming that it was resurrecting."

Traci shook her head. "And I thought my family was weird," she said, trying to be funny.

It fell a little flat and on impulse Cindy reached out and hugged her.

"Is your great aunt still alive? Maybe she could provide some perspective," Jeremiah suggested.

"Unfortunately no. She died when I was in college. And even if she hadn't I'm not sure she would have been that helpful. After the whole Easter dinner incident she pretty much shunned our side of the family."

Jeremiah's phone rang and he pulled it out. "Hi, Marie, what's up?"

Cindy could hear the other woman on the phone. Her voice was shrill and hurried as if there was something terribly wrong.

"Slow down. When did this happen? I see. Have the police been notified? What did they say? Okay, we'll hold a vigil for her tomorrow morning. Yes. I'll be there."

He hung up the phone and she could tell from the look on his face that it was bad news. She could feel her heart begin to pound. "What is it? What's wrong?"

"One of the girls from the synagogue just ran away from home."

10

Both Cindy and Traci expressed their concern with how terrible that was. Jeremiah shook his head as he put away his phone. "We'd all kind of seen the writing on the wall for the last few months. Meghan had been desperately unhappy at home and nothing anyone did could seem to make it better. I know her older sister, Sarah, pretty well and I know she's been struggling to understand Meghan, and be there for her, but it's been hard on everyone."

"What do you need to do?" Cindy asked.

"There's nothing I can do right now but pray for her. We'll be holding a prayer vigil at the synagogue in the morning for friends and family to come and unite together hoping that our prayers will help bring her home. The police have been notified and they're keeping an eye out for her. Hopefully one of them will pick her up somewhere and take her home none the worse for wear."

"I still wish I knew what happened to Lizzie," Traci said in distress. "She took her toothbrush which means she had to go wherever she went on purpose, right?"

"It would seem like it," Cindy said. "You and I have both been kidnapped and no one gave us time to pack a toiletry bag," she said.

Traci stared at her for a moment and then, to Jeremiah's surprise, started giggling. "You're right. The thought's absurd."

"I know," Cindy said with a grin.

He shook his head. Cindy always managed to bring out the best even in dark situations. It was one of her gifts.

"Hey, you never told us what happened at the doctor's office," he realized.

"Oh," Cindy said, rolling her eyes.

"This must be good," Traci commented.

"The doctor ran a bunch of tests and what he came up with was a minor allergy to ragweed and a major allergy to acacia trees."

"That's it?" he asked.

"That's it. Weird, huh? I was expecting dust, fungus, witchcraft, you know to be allergic to one of those."

Traci belted out a laugh this time so loud it even startled her.

"Sorry," she said, covering her mouth sheepishly.

"I live to amuse," Cindy countered.

"Then long live you," Traci said, raising her glass of orange juice.

He and Cindy did the same in the impromptu toast.

"Acacia trees. Are there many around here?" Traci asked.

Cindy shrugged. "The doctor said they're more prevalent up in Northern California, but they are down here along the coastal areas as well."

"So, what was eau de acacia tree doing in that basement?" Traci asked. "I mean, if that really was what set off your allergy attack."

"I have no idea," Cindy said. "I mean, I noticed a weird smell in the basement, but you know it was musty and gross down in there and it could have been anything really. I mean, I wouldn't even know what acacia smells like to be able to tell if they had some weird air deodorizer going with that in it."

Jeremiah shook his head.

"What?" she asked.

"You honestly think someone put a room deodorizer in that house?"

"I know, it sounds ridiculous, but how else do you explain it?"

He couldn't frankly. Every possible answer that came to mind was more ridiculous than the one before it so he finally gave up.

"You don't think they use acacia in any kind of weird rituals, do you?" Traci asked suddenly.

They both turned to stare at her.

"That might actually make sense," Cindy said. She hopped to her feet.

"Where are you going?" Jeremiah asked.

"To borrow Mark's computer for a minute. I can't believe I didn't think about looking it up earlier."

"In what time? You've been pretty busy since your doctor's visit earlier," Traci said.

Almost as if compelled to do so they both stood up and followed her into the office. Jeremiah hesitated in the doorway. The last time he'd been in that room he'd had to come clean with Mark about his past and try to tell Cindy that he had to leave. The memories came flooding back to him. That had been a terrible day. Yet, they had gotten past it and here they were again. Once Mark made it home the circle of crazy would be complete.

Cindy did a quick web search and then started scrolling through links before clicking on one. The color slowly drained out of her face as she read.

"What is it?" Traci asked.

"You were right. It is used in rituals," Cindy answered.

"What kind of rituals?" Jeremiah asked sharply.

"From what I'm seeing it has a strong association with death in early Egyptian, Jewish, and Christian culture. It's also a symbol of immortality and initiation through resurrection."

She scrolled down the page farther while both Jeremiah and Traci leaned in trying to get a better look.

"Ah! It says here that it is burned on charcoal in rituals to enhance someone's individual power."

"All of those are bad things," Jeremiah said softly.

"It's possible someone was trying to do an initiation through resurrection spell or a power spell," Cindy said. "If they were burning the acacia that could have been that strange odor, and I could have had that reaction to it."

"If it was still that present, then the police couldn't have gotten there that long after the killer left," Jeremiah pointed out.

"If the killer even left," Cindy countered.

"What do you mean?"

"At one point I could swear I heard someone whispering to me, a voice outside my head. What if the killer was there but in a hidden room or something and the acacia was still burning?" Cindy asked.

"A hidden room, how likely is that?" he asked.

"I don't know, how likely was it to find a ritualized human sacrifice in a basement in a house in California?" she challenged.

Meanwhile next to them Traci had gone ash white and was shaking.

"What's wrong?" he asked, turning to her and putting a steadying hand on her arm.

"It says you can burn it to gain power. That's what Lizzie was obsessed with. Power. She'd had a taste of it and she wanted more. I warned her that it would never be enough, but she didn't want to hear it."

Cindy reached out and grabbed her hand. "I'm sure Lizzie had nothing to do with that girl's death."

"How can you be sure?" Traci asked.

"I can't, but I have a hard time believing a sister of yours would be capable of something like that."

Traci nodded slowly, but didn't say anything.

"We're going to get to the bottom of this, and we'll get Lizzie back, you'll see," Cindy said, giving her a brilliant smile.

They heard the front door open and a minute later Mark joined them in the office. He looked around at all of them. "What did I miss?" he asked.

Traci threw her arms around his neck and burst into tears.

It ended up being a late night with the four of them exchanging information, theories, everything. Mark was dragging come morning, but had agreed to meet Trina for a late breakfast to confab and strategize.

When he got to the restaurant he realized he'd missed a call on his phone from the Sweater Girl. He listened to her message and she apologized, but said that no one else had the phone numbers of those other two people. That was not the news he was looking for.

He slid into the booth at the restaurant and a minute later gave the waitress his order. Once Trina had ordered and the waitress had headed off, he turned and looked at her.

"By the way, thanks for the tip last night. Apparently it was a good night to hold a coven meeting. I found the wiccan coven I was looking for. They seemed harmless enough actually, so I'm not sure they're the wiccans you're here to chase down."

"I'm not here chasing wiccans," Trina said.

"Then with all due respect, who are you here chasing?" Mark asked.

She picked up her coffee, took a sip of it, then set it down. "Witches."

"There's a difference?" he asked.

She narrowed her eyes slightly. "Yes, the former is a religious group practicing an earth religion and bound by a certain moral code."

"Which would be what, exactly?"

"It goes 'and it harm none, do what thou will'. There is also a belief, a warning principle, that whatever you put out into the universe comes back on you sevenfold. So, to put out anything evil would be to visit it back on yourself seven times worse. They respect the earth, draw power from it."

"So, overly religious hippies," he said.

Now she was outright glaring at him. He had no idea if she herself was a wiccan, but he was certainly getting under her skin. That's what he wanted to do, people often revealed more about themselves, their knowledge, and their intentions when you egged them on.

"Moving on," she said tartly. "Witches, specifically dark witches, don't necessarily practice a religion of any sort, what they practice are a bunch of spells and magic that they think will bring them power and personal gain. Their rituals can range from the merely dark to the obscene."

Her words chilled him to the bone. It wasn't so much the description of their rituals but her description of the kind of people that fell into that trap. It must have shown on his face because Trina leaned forward.

"What's wrong?" she asked.

He was the one looking to get answers, not give them, but he felt an overwhelming urge to be honest with her. It made sense. After all, if this was her area of expertise maybe she could help shed some light on things. And if there was even a remote chance she could help find Lizzie he had to try.

"It's my sister-in-law, Lizzie. A couple of years ago she announced to the family that she was going to become a wiccan. She told us what you did, about it being a religion and it was about harming no one and being a responsible citizen and getting in touch with nature, a lot of that."

"And that caused a problem?"

"No, actually. My wife's family isn't religious. Neither was mine. So, while it seemed odd to everyone, it wasn't like anybody was overly upset about her choice. Honestly, the way she talked about it, it just sounded like a lot of hippie talk to me which actually fit with her personality. It was like she was taking it one step further and finding a religion in it instead of just a lifestyle."

"Hence your correlating what I was saying with wiccans all being hippies?"

"Exactly," Mark admitted. "That and I was provoking you a bit," he said, shocked to hear himself say it.

"I know. But back to Lizzie. I take it something changed?" Trina guessed.

"Yes, after a few months she started to change. Her wardrobe, her attitude, everything became what I can only call 'dark'. I teased her at one family gathering that she looked like a Goth and she got offended. Then when she was talking to my wife, Traci, she started telling her that she was learning so many new things and that she was getting things out of it. She was talking about doing spells to get more power. She even said she'd put a curse on her ex-boyfriend."

"Yeah, definitely not playing by the Wiccan rulebook anymore. It sounds like she was falling in with a dangerous crowd," Trina said.

Mark nodded. "Traci told her she was worried about her, and Lizzie pretty much cut her out of her life at that point. Traci tried to reach out several times after that, but nothing. Their older sister Amber retained some contact, but even that was a lot less than it once was, and if Traci was going to be at a party or something that pretty much made it a guarantee that Lizzie wouldn't show."

"That's actually not a bad thing," Trina said softly.

"In what universe is that not a bad thing?" Mark asked bluntly.

"Her discomfort around Traci indicates that deep down she knew that what she was doing was wrong, and she didn't want people in her life who would remind her of that fact. If she'd gone completely over to the dark side she wouldn't have cared at all what Traci thought or said."

"So, maybe there's hope for her?" Mark asked. For Traci's sake he wanted to believe so.

"There could be."

Mark cleared his throat. There was one burning question that needed to be asked. "Do you think it's possible that she's involved with whoever killed Cheyenne and Michelle?"

Trina picked up her cup of coffee and took a deep breath. "I think she might be, yes."

Mark swore softly.

"It's possible that she doesn't realize what her new friends, her new coven are really up to. She could be just a pawn who doesn't even know the extent of what the others are doing."

"Yeah, but what are the odds of that?" Mark said with a shake of his head.

"Actually, not horrible. I've seen it before. Several times actually. A couple of powerful and persuasive dark witches have a goal that requires more people to accomplish. They recruit, oftentimes going after the disenfranchised or unempowered. Even frustrated Wiccans who wish they had more power or more control or have a desire for something that would break their own belief structure can be targets. It could be that's exactly what happened to Lizzie. For all we know they preyed on her anger toward her ex-boyfriend. Any chance we know who he is, by the way? I'd like to talk to him."

"We don't, but I'll check with Amber and see if she ever knew his name." He found himself pulling out his phone. "Actually, let me do that right now."

"Excellent," Trina said, sitting back in her seat and taking another sip of her coffee.

Fortunately Amber picked up on the second ring. "Mark, have you found Lizzie?" she asked, voice full of worry.

"No, but we're working on it. Listen, not last Christmas but the one before I think it was she had recently broken up with an ex-boyfriend."

"I remember, she told me she put a curse on the guy. Have you ever heard anything so ridiculous?"

"Yeah, well, any chance you know who he was, a name, a picture?"

"Let me think. She brought him over for dinner once before they broke up. He had reddish colored hair. His name was...Samuel, that was it."

"Did you hear a last name?"

"I think she said, but I can't honestly remember."

"That's okay," Mark said, struggling to keep the frustration out of his voice. "Do you know how they met?"

"Yes, I think he was in her Wicca coven."

"Thanks, I'll keep you posted," he said before hanging up. He wished he had known that last night.

"He was from her coven?"

"Good ears," Mark commented.

Trina shrugged.

"Only there were no guys there last night with red hair and I got the impression that all the members were present and accounted for."

"So, maybe one of them knows more about him."

"That's what I'm hoping," he said as he pulled his notebook out of his pocket and looked up Sweater Girl's phone number. Fortunately she picked up right away, too.

"Hi, this is Detective Walters, I got your message."

"I'm sorry I couldn't get any contact information for you," she said.

"It's okay."

"Did you tell the other officers to be on the lookout for black cats?"

"No, but I will. I actually had a couple of follow up questions for you, though" he said.

"What are they?" she asked.

"I'm trying to locate an ex-boyfriend of Lizzie's. I think he might have been part of the coven. His name was Samuel and apparently he had red hair. Do you know him?"

"I know him," she said, her voice tight.

"Is he still a member of the coven?"

"Not really, no."

It seemed like an odd answer. "Do you by any chance know where I can find him?"

"Yes. At the hospital here in Pine Springs. He's been in a coma for almost two years."

11

"Whoa, what happened to him?"

"No one knows. We all did our best, tried everything we could think of, but nothing helped him. We finally had to give up. It was shortly after that Lizzie left the coven."

"Do you know what his last name is?"

"Bannerman."

"Thank you."

"You're welcome. Detective, I hope you find Lizzie. She used to be nice. I wish I knew what it was that happened to her."

"Me, too," he said before hanging up. *Used to be nice.* Even her former coven had noticed the change in her.

"So, Lizzie left the coven shortly after her ex-boyfriend, Samuel Bannerman, ended up in a coma. Apparently, he's still in the coma."

Trina nodded as though she wasn't particularly surprised. She drained her coffee, tossed some bills on the table, and stood up. "Let's go visit him, shall we?"

Mark followed her out to the parking lot. "We'll take my car," he said.

She nodded and a minute later they were on the road. "I didn't mean to open up so much back there," he said, feeling a bit embarrassed as he thought about it.

"It's okay. I guess I have one of those faces. People tend to want to tell me things."

"That must make the job easier."

"It can," she admitted. "And in this case, I'm sure it will. If we're going to solve this we can't be holding out on each other. If you hadn't told me about Lizzie then we wouldn't know to go visit Samuel."

"Yeah, a lot of good this is probably going to do us. Guy's been in a coma for a couple of years, I don't think he'll have much to say."

"You might be surprised," she said cryptically.

"You're a little weird, you know that?"

She laughed. "You're not the first to think so, but most people don't actually say it."

"Well, you know, in the spirit of not holding back."

"Funny."

"So, how many cases like this one have you worked?"

"A few. It's always tricky. The most recent one was in New Orleans, boy that was a mess."

"The city of superstition? I bet you couldn't swing a black cat without hitting a dark witch," he joked.

"That's one of the things that's bothering me."

"What?"

"What was that girl from the coven saying about looking out for black cats?"

"Apparently both her cat and her neighbor's cat went missing and they were both black cats. It is getting close to Halloween and there are a lot of sick people out there. I hate to say it, but I think something like that happens every year."

"It does, unfortunately, but these are people who would have been aware of the danger, and presumably, keeping closer tabs on their cats because of it. I just find it odd that two people had their cats stolen on the same night."

"They never said stolen."

"No, but I'd be willing to bet they were."

"The coroner did say that he found some cat fur at the first crime scene. I had just assumed that it was old or from stray cats breaking in to forage for mice."

"I think where this case is concerned it's better to suspect everything and assume nothing," she told him.

"The voice of experience?"

"Exactly."

"Whatever you say."

A few minutes later they were pulling up outside the hospital. Inside they were directed to a ward where there were a couple of patients in comas. None of them, though, had been there more than a couple of days with the exception of Samuel.

They had been standing at his bedside looking at him for less than a minute when a doctor appeared, having been alerted to their presence.

"Detective, Agent," he said, shaking their hands. "I'm Doctor Wilson. How can I help?"

"We'd like to know more about this patient," Trina said.

"He was brought in almost two years ago in the exact condition you see him in now. He was already in a coma when his roommate found him and called an ambulance."

"What caused it?" Mark asked.

"That's the strange part. We can't tell. We've run every test possible on him and medically speaking, there's no obvious cause. He didn't play sports, hadn't received any bumps to the head, hadn't suffered from oxygen deprivation. They had been in the apartment all day, studying for finals. Apparently he had laid down on the couch before dinner to take a nap. When the pizza got there his roommate tried to wake him and couldn't. After trying for a minute with no luck he called 911."

"It's not normal for someone to just take a nap and not wake up," Mark said.

"No, it isn't, but, like I said, all tests have proved inconclusive. We have no idea why this man slipped into a coma and no idea why he's stayed there."

"If you can, Doctor, we'd like to get his roommate's name and contact information."

"I'll give you what I have, but the guy graduated college in the spring. He had come by about once a week just to check in. I was there on his last visit. He'd been accepted to a graduate school back east. I think he left a number, asked to be notified if there was ever any change. I'll see if I can find it for you."

"We appreciate it," Trina said.

The doctor walked off, ostensibly to track down the number for them. Trina turned and put her hand on Samuel's forehead.

"What are you doing?" Mark asked.

"Thinking," she said.

"You've got a strange way of thinking."

"Would you be quiet for a second?"

She was getting weirder and it made Mark uneasy. He took a step backward even as he found himself wondering what her deal was. He watched as she closed her eyes. She kept her hand on Samuel's forehead and her lips were moving ever so slightly. Maybe she was saying a prayer over him or something. He knew some people did that.

Finally she turned, removing her hand from the guy as she did so. "Do any of the local churches have faith healers?" she asked.

"Uh, I'm sure I wouldn't know," he said, taken aback. She must have been praying for the guy. "Why?"

"Can you find out for me? I want to get some people out here to pray over this guy."

"Seriously?" he asked.

She raised one eyebrow. "You heard the doctor, medical science has no idea what's wrong with him or how to fix him. Don't you think it's time to let someone else have a try?"

"Um, okay. I know some church people. I'll ask them."

"Ask them now," she said, her voice lowering slightly.

He found himself pulling his phone out of his pocket almost before he knew what he was doing. He called Cindy at her work number.

"Hello?"

"Cindy, Mark. Strange question. Is anyone over there at First Shepherd into faith healing?"

She paused. "We've got a prayer chain and several of the people in it are definitely prayer warriors. I've never heard any of them claim to be healers, though."

"Could you ask around and find out for me? There's a guy here in the hospital who's been in a coma for a couple of years. Doctors have no clue why. The F.B.I. agent I'm working with on this wants to see if any of the local churches have someone they can send out to pray over him, you know, just to cover our bases, I guess."

"Well, I know I can send some people out to pray for him."

"That might be good enough," Trina spoke up, clearly overhearing.

"Good, could you do that, sooner rather than later? His name is Samuel Bannerman."

"Okay, I'll have some people out there this evening."

"Thanks."

He hung up the phone.

"She's a good friend," Trina noted.

"One of the best. Even when something scares her silly she's still there, trying to help."

"For a man who's not religious you seem to have surrounded yourself with a circle of people who are."

"Yeah, it's funny how things work out sometimes," Mark noted.

"I want to be here when they're praying over him," she said.

"Add your voice to theirs?"

"Something like that," she said with a smile.

The doctor came back and handed them a piece of paper with the contact information for the roommate. Mark called, but had to leave a message on the man's voicemail.

"Some people from First Shepherd will be coming this evening to pray over this man," Trina informed the doctor.

He nodded. "Not much on prayer myself, but I have seen it do things I couldn't explain, and this poor guy could use all the help he can get."

Cindy made one phone call and was able to set in motion the prayer chain. Twenty minutes later she got a call back saying that about fifteen people would be there at 7 p.m. to pray for Samuel. She called back Mark and let him know. That done, she got back to work trying to get the information to Geanie that the other woman needed to put together the Sunday bulletin.

Wednesdays were the day that she put them together for the pastors to look over on Thursday before they got printed on Friday. Some weeks it felt a bit like an assembly line, but at least it got done. It was one job Cindy was grateful that Geanie took care of. She always managed to find enough room for all of the announcements without having to change the format or anything. Whenever she was out on vacation it was the one part of her job that Cindy dreaded doing.

She had just about sent Geanie everything when the phone on her desk rang. She could tell by the tone that it was an internal line. She glanced over and saw that Dave was calling. It rang a second time and then stopped.

She pulled her hand back and glanced over at Geanie. "Who was it?" the other woman asked, looking up, forehead crinkling in concern.

"Dave," Cindy said, already standing up and heading for the door.

They had a policy that two rings and a hang up meant that someone needed assistance, but couldn't necessarily talk on the phone for some reason. They used it kind of like an emergency paging system, but it was rare that it actually happened.

She made her way quickly to the youth room where he had his office. Once inside she saw that he was in the office sitting on the couch next to a teen girl who had buried her head in his shoulder. He looked up at Cindy as she entered the room, his eyes full of distress.

"Brenda, Cindy's here," he said.

The girl turned and Cindy recognized Brenda Parker, one of the highschoolers that she actually knew. The girl's family was desperately poor and she was the only one of them who came to church. A couple of years earlier Cindy and some of the high school girls had been delivering Thanksgiving dinner to the Parker family, not realizing until it was too late that the reason Brenda insisted on staying in the car was because it was actually her family that they were delivering the charitable meal to.

Brenda stood up and crossed over to Cindy and threw her arms around her as she continued to sob.

Bewildered, Cindy held the girl while she cried and looked at Dave, wondering what on earth was wrong.

"She just found out that a friend of hers, Cheyenne, was killed a couple of days ago," Mark said softly.

Cindy's heart constricted when she heard that and she could feel tears forming in her own eyes. Brenda's life was hard enough without having to deal with such a tragedy at her age. Cheyenne was the girl who had been murdered in the basement of that terrible house. It wasn't even like she'd been killed in a car accident. No, what had happened to Brenda's friend had been unspeakable and there was a good chance that Brenda would carry the scars of that the rest of her life.

Cindy couldn't hold back her own tears. She knew what it was like to have sudden death rip away childhood innocence. They sat back down on the couch and cried together. Cindy quietly, tears streaming down her face, Brenda sobbing with wild abandon, the cries of a breaking heart.

Dave just hovered over them, distress on his face.

After several minutes the sobs started to let up and finally Cindy heard Brenda say a single word.

"Why?"

She looked up at Dave, at a loss as to what to say. He crouched down next to them and put a hand on Brenda's shoulder.

"Evil exists in this world, Brenda. It's a terrible thing, and things happen that make no sense to us. Sometimes we get answers, but other times we have to live with the uncertainty. God knows what happened to Cheyenne, and He knows why. All I can say is that if it's important for you to know why it happened, why her, then He will let you know. And if it's not important for you to know the answer, then you need to trust that He has a reason for not telling you."

Cindy wasn't sure that was what she would have gone with, but then again, she had struggled with that same question over her sister's death for years. Maybe if someone had been able to say to her what Dave had just said to Brenda it would have helped. She didn't know.

"I know it feels like the world is ending right now," she said softly. "But it's not. You've had someone taken from you, and I'm so sorry you had to experience that, but for every great loss in our life there is healing, for everyone that leaves us, no matter why or how, someone new comes into our lives."

Sometimes that process could take years. It had with her, but if Brenda was open to the possibility maybe she wouldn't close herself off from people for years like Cindy had and her healing could happen faster.

Dave nodded to her. He thought she had said something right which was a bit of a relief.

Brenda sat up slowly, drying her eyes. "I got your shirt all wet," she said dully.

"It's no big deal," Cindy said.

"Did Cheyenne go to your school?" Dave asked, pulling up his chair and sitting down.

"She used to, but her mom pulled her out to start homeschooling her at the end of last year. She was upset about it, too. She was looking forward to some of the senior activities. Not that her mom would have let her do any of them. She was always real strict. I was Cheyenne's only friend. We still managed to hang out sometimes the last few months, but it was hard."

Cindy knew from talking with Mark that Cheyenne's parents hadn't been able to shed any light on her death. She realized, though, that she might have an opportunity to find out more than he had, but she didn't want to hurt Brenda more in the process. She said a quick prayer for guidance and the right words.

"Brenda, I know the police are trying to find out what happened to her, but they're having a bit of a hard time finding out anything about her from her parents."

"Of course they are. Her dad's never around and her mom refused to see anything but a little clone of herself. Sometimes I think that's why she was so hard on Cheyenne. That, and she was afraid Cheyenne would end up like her sister."

Cindy blinked, latching on to that little bit of information. She schooled herself to be calm, gentle, and not push too hard. "She had an older sister?"

"Yeah, Lacey. She's in college. She's a psycho, a total mess."

"How so?"

"When we were Freshmen and Lacey was a Senior she was always getting into trouble, dating guys who were just scary, you know. She smoked and drank at school even.

She always talked about how much she hated her family, hated Pine Springs and one day she was going to be a big shot and have everything she ever wanted. Because of her teachers were always hard on Cheyenne at first until they realized that she was nothing like her sister."

"Did they get along?"

Brenda shook her head. "Lacey hated Cheyenne because she thought their parents loved her more and she was always picking on her, doing things to hurt her that Cheyenne could never prove, or was too afraid to talk about. She was so glad when Lacey moved into the dorms. Even though she was only twenty minutes away she never came back home, not even for Christmas I don't think. She didn't get that their parents were so hard on Cheyenne, so strict and mean because they didn't want her to be like Lacey. I always thought they loved Lacey best because they always gave her a pass. Instead of punishing her, they'd just get stricter with Cheyenne. It was unfair, you know?"

Brenda dashed away fresh tears that had started to flow.

Cindy's brain was working overtime. she had one more question she wanted to ask, but she had to be delicate about it. "You said that Lacey would do things to Cheyenne. You don't think she'd ever really hurt her, do you?"

Brenda looked up and there was anger blazing in her eyes. "Cheyenne had two broken fingers the last quarter of our Freshman year. She told everyone that she'd tripped off a curb, but I knew the truth. Lacey broke them because she was mad at her. She just grabbed them and snapped them like she was snapping twigs, and she didn't even care. And she told Cheyenne that if she told the truth she'd break the rest of her fingers. Cheyenne believed her. Lacey wouldn't hesitate to hurt her. I wouldn't even be surprised to find out Lacey killed her."

12

"Think what you're saying," Dave urged Brenda after he and Cindy exchanged a look.

"I don't have to think about it. Lacey was mean and scary and she hurt Cheyenne a lot. No one will tell me how she died, just that she was murdered. And when I heard that, the first thing I thought was that it had to be Lacey. Cheyenne was so quiet and timid, no one else would ever want to hurt her for any reason."

Brenda began crying again and Cindy put her arms around her. "Thank you for telling us," Cindy said softly.

"If I can help in any way I will," Brenda said, her words muffled.

"You've already helped quite a bit," Cindy reassured her.

It took another hour before Brenda was ready to go home. Dave offered to drive her so she wouldn't have to take the bus back, but she insisted on taking the bus. "My family doesn't really understand why I come to church," she said sheepishly.

"Well, we understand, and we're glad that you do," Cindy said, giving her a smile even though her heart was still breaking for her.

"Thank you. You've always been so nice," Brenda said.

Cindy felt bad. Her interactions with the girl had been few and far between and Brenda clearly needed more love and attention in her life. Dave did his best, but he was only one man with a hundred kids to look out for. She vowed that she'd start paying more attention, particularly to the ones that God brought across her path.

"I'll walk you to the bus stop," Cindy said.

"Thank you."

It was just up the street a block, but Cindy was happy to go with her. They walked in silence and then Cindy stayed while she waited for the bus. When she saw it coming up the street she turned and looked at Brenda. "Would you like to go out to lunch Sunday after church?"

Brenda hesitated and Cindy thought for a moment that she had overstepped. "That sounds really nice, but I promised I'd help put together the haunted house."

Cindy blinked in surprise. She couldn't believe that given what she was going through that would even be on Brenda's mind at the moment. If she'd been in her shoes the last thing she'd want to do was be reminded of horror and death. She took a deep breath, reminding herself that Brenda was much older than she had been when her sister died. Of course she would view things differently.

The bus pulled up and Brenda got on. When she reached the top step she turned around. "I'd be free for lunch the week after," she said, her voice hopeful.

"You're on," Cindy assured her.

Brenda nodded and disappeared into the back of the bus.

By the time Mark made it into the office there was a message for him from the coroner. He called the man back, eager to get some news.

"Hey, it's Mark. What did you find?" he asked when the man picked up.

"You're not going to like it."

Mark winced. "That doesn't sound good."

"Cause of death on both girls is a little iffy, but I'm having to go with heart attacks."

"What? In girls that young that makes no sense."

"I know, and I did tox screens to see if they could have been administered drugs that would have caused the heart attacks, but they came back clean. I honestly believe that both these girls died of fright."

"You're kidding, right?"

"Wish I was. I'm not."

"They were scared to death?"

"It can happen and here it appears that it did."

"What am I supposed to do with that?" Mark asked.

"I don't know. I didn't find anything else really of interest, no trace chemicals, soil samples that would be from someplace other than where they died. Only thing I found was some cat hair near the first body in the basement, but you already knew that."

"What type of cat hair was it again?"

"Medium length. Black."

Mark sat up straight. "Did you find any cat hair around the second body?"

"No, but she was staked out in a grassy field in the open. If it was there at one point it could have been blown away by a breeze. It could have even been there and just not noticeable in the grass."

"Was there cat hair on either of the bodies?"

"Nope. No human hair either other than their own. I'm telling you, these are two of the cleanest corpses I've ever seen. I don't know what to tell you beyond what I already have."

"Okay, thanks, keep me updated," Mark said before hanging up. This case was getting creepier and creepier. If the coroner was going to put scared to death on his official reports, though, there was nothing for Mark to do but run with that theory. The question then became who or what could have possibly frightened both girls badly enough to have killed them?

Jeremiah was sitting in his office half-staring into space. The early morning prayer vigil had been difficult to get through. There had been so many worried, anxious people there and he'd led them in prayers for two hours longer than he had intended. It was disheartening that the police still hadn't found Meghan and he was beginning to worry that she might already be out of the city and on her way to becoming one of the nameless, lost children that populated the streets of Los Angeles.

There wasn't anything more he could do about it, though. He had put it in G-d's hands and he had to trust that everything would come out right and the prodigal would return home. His office phone rang, startling him out of his thoughts.

Jeremiah picked it up. "Hello?"

"Rabbi! Dave Wyman."

"What can I do for you Wildman?"

"Well, the list is long, but actually I'm calling because a bunch of the kids are meeting at the church tonight and I thought it might be a good time for you to come out and start teaching them how to scare the pants off people. Metaphorically speaking."

Jeremiah rubbed his eyes. It was the last thing he wanted to do, but he really did need to get it over with so that the youth pastor could let it alone.

"What time?"

"Six."

"I'll be there," he promised.

"You're the best!"

As Jeremiah hung up the phone he couldn't help but wonder how he got himself into these situations.

His cell went off, and he pulled it out of his pocket in disgust. He just wanted a few minutes of peace to himself, but apparently that was too much to ask for. It turned out that Mark was calling.

"Did you have a chance to look up those symbols that were marked on the bodies?" he asked without preamble.

"No. I'll do that tonight supposing I survive my teaching course over at the church."

"What teaching course?"

"I get to teach a bunch of teenagers how to run a scary haunted house."

He could swear he heard Mark laughing, but it was muffled. After a moment the detective said, "I'd pay to see that."

"You might, but you won't. No grownups allowed, except me."

"Too bad."

Jeremiah sighed. "I can tell you right now what the Hebrew words meant."

"What?"

"There was a hodgepodge of them. They were isolated from each other so there was no way to tell if there was supposed to be an order or a rational connection between them."

"That's fine, I'm ready, lay them on me."

"Death. Darkness. Power. Initiate. Resurrection. Life Eternal. Sacrifice. Offering. Cost."

"Great. Half of those sound like they go really well with the meaning of acacia that Cindy discovered last night."

"If they really were burning acacia in that basement that would make sense."

Mark was quiet for a moment. "I need to go back down there."

Jeremiah could hear the fear in the other man's voice.

"I'm not sure that's such a good idea."

"Neither am I, but do you have a better one?"

"Not yet, give me a moment."

"I'll give you all day if it would help. Trust me, going back there is the last thing I want to do, but I have a feeling we missed something."

"You're not alone in that feeling."

"I promised Traci I wouldn't go back in that house. She got really freaked out when I told her about it that first night. It was like she was scared that something was going to happen to me in that house."

"Maybe something is going to happen to you in that house," Jeremiah said quietly.

Mark swore. "You really know just what to say to make a guy feel better."

"I'm not going to discount what Traci felt. I've seen women's intuition work before."

"So have I which just puts me that much more on edge," Mark admitted. "I hate this whole bloody case."

"At least the press haven't gotten hold of it yet."

"That in and of itself is a miracle and I'm not questioning it, I'm just giving thanks for it."

"Sound plan."

"Tell you what, you want to go into that house for me and poke around?"

Jeremiah paused for a moment. "Do you want to teach a bunch of high-schoolers the best way to scare their friends and families?"

"No, but I'd still pay money to watch you do it."

"I bet."

"Okay, so no job switching for us. Probably just as well. Nerves like yours you'd probably go all to pieces in that house."

The Detective was trying to make a joke but his own anxiety caused it to come out flat. "Be careful, Mark," Jeremiah told him.

"You, too, man. Let me know if there's anything I need to know."

"Same with you."

Jeremiah hung up the phone and he wrestled for a moment with feelings of guilt. There was no way he wanted to go back into that house again. If Traci had really had that strong a reaction, though, as a friend he shouldn't let Mark go in alone.

He glanced at the clock. He had almost five hours before he had to go teach that class and there was no way he was going to be able to focus on work. With a sigh he got up and left his office, locking the door behind him.

Marie glanced up, brow furrowing.

"I'm going to be out the rest of the afternoon," he told her.

She narrowed her eyes, but didn't say anything which was just as well. If she'd accused him of sneaking off to spend time with Cindy, or whatever colorful new and inappropriate nickname she came up with for her this time then he couldn't be held responsible for what he would say in return.

As soon as he hit the parking lot he pulled his cell back out. The Detective picked up right away.

"Mark, hold up. I'm coming with you."

"I knew you were a crazy son-of-a-gun."

"What is it you say? Takes one to know one?"

"That's about right."

After a brief discussion they opted to meet at the house itself.

When Jeremiah arrived he was surprised to see a woman in a dark suit standing next to Mark's car. Jeremiah gave him a questioning look as he walked over to them.

"I decided to bring back up. Trina works for the F.B.I. and investigates all this cult crap. She hasn't had the privilege yet of going into the house."

"I guess it's your lucky day," Jeremiah said, keeping his voice neutral.

"Jeremiah, right?" she asked, extending her hand.

He shook it. "Nice to meet you. Now let's get this over with."

Truth was, knowing there was an agent there with Mark, Jeremiah had to fight down the urge to get in his car and drive straight back to the synagogue. He thought of Traci, though, and knew that he owed it to her to try and make sure her husband stayed alive and in one piece.

"Ugly building, isn't it?" Trina asked.

"You don't know the half of it," Mark muttered.

They went up the steps to the porch one at a time, cautious so as not to fall through the rotting wood.

As Mark opened the door every instinct Jeremiah had screamed at him to not go inside. Mark began to step forward, but Trina stopped him with a hand on his shoulder.

"Do you mind if I go first?"

"I'd be happy to let you go first, middle, and last," Mark said.

Jeremiah noticed that the Detective had already begun to sweat like he had been in the house the other day. His own stomach was clenching making it feel like his intestines were tying themselves up in knots.

Trina stood for a moment on the threshold and she slowly waved her hand through the air from left to right. He had no idea what she was looking for, but clearly she did because a moment later she nodded and stepped inside.

Mark followed her and Jeremiah brought up the rear. It was not a position he fancied. The few times he'd worked with teams back in the old days he'd always preferred point. What was sneaking up behind him was always what worried him which was why he always wanted to know who or what was back there.

Without being told Trina managed to make a beeline for the kitchen and the door leading down to the basement.

"I don't remember closing that door," Mark muttered.

"You probably didn't," Trina said.

She held her hand up to the door and paused a moment.

Jeremiah strained his senses but he didn't hear anything. He did have that tickling sensation on the back of his neck, though, that always warned him when he was being watched. He swiveled around but could see no one. He turned back, trying to block out the sensation lest it drive him crazy.

Trina took her hand and ran it down the edge of the door frame for a good two feet before she finally grabbed the doorknob with her other hand and twisted it open.

A blast of foul, dank air radiated outward, potent enough to drive both he and Mark back a couple of steps. Trina stood her ground, though. She had her head cocked to the side as though listening for something. He still didn't hear anything.

There was no way Mark was going down into that basement. Not a chance. Not for all the money in the world. The dread he had felt in that house a couple of days before was somehow back tenfold. Maybe it was because it was just the three of them and there wasn't an army of police officers scouring the entire building. Maybe it was because he had this creeping feeling of terror that he might find Lizzie's body down there this time. Or maybe it was because all this talk of dark witches was finally starting to get to him.

I don't believe in the supernatural, he told himself sternly. That should have made him feel better yet somehow it seemed cold comfort when he knew for a fact that the woman in front of him and the man behind him both did.

Maybe I'm the one that's wrong.

The thought chilled him to the bone. He had always taken comfort in being an atheist, in believing that this life was all you got and there was no one out there watching out for you so you had to watch out for yourself and those you loved. At the moment, though, he'd give anything to have Jeremiah's faith or Cindy's. He wanted to believe that God was real and that He was going to look out for Mark.

I promised Traci I wouldn't come back here.

He was sweating profusely even though it wasn't warm. He'd had some close calls in his years on the force, but he'd never been so utterly and totally convinced that he was about to die. He was insane for being here. He should have listened to his wife. She knew, somehow she knew. He didn't know how she knew, but she had told him he shouldn't come back here and he had been a fool not to listen.

I promised Traci. I shouldn't have broken that promise.

"I can't do this."

"Yes, you can. Don't give into the fear," Trina said. "That's what they want you to do."

He had no idea who the "they" were she was referencing, but if he'd had a white flag he would have held it high and run out of the building. He felt Jeremiah's hand descend suddenly on his shoulder. He jumped, but then felt himself relax slightly. A humorous saying he'd once seen popped to mind and he mentally altered it to fit his current situation.

Yay though I walk through the valley of the shadow of death, I will fear no evil, for I'm walking with the meanest son of a gun in the whole darn valley.

And somehow that made him smile and the tightness he'd been feeling in his chest eased up.

"You don't have to do this," Jeremiah whispered.

It was an out. He knew it. He wanted to take it. The man who had spent his life hiding in shadows was telling him it was okay to retreat, and deep down he knew he should listen. Even if Trina did think that would be giving in to fear. What was it they said? Discretion was the better part of valor.

He wasn't a coward. He knew that. And now he knew that the rabbi wouldn't blame him for turning tail. Yet when Trina switched on the flashlight she had been carrying and led the way down the stairs, he found himself following.

The darkness pressed in around, thick and close, and the momentary relief he'd felt at realizing who he was walking through it with vanished. Twice he practically stepped on the back of Trina's heels in an effort to stay close to the meager light that was all that was keeping the darkness at bay.

They were nearly at the bottom of the stairs and the hair on the back of his neck was standing on end. He found himself looking into the darkness, imagining what terrors it held. Even though Cheyenne's body was gone Mark felt like he could still see her lying there on the floor of the basement, eyes wide in terror.

That's what killed her. Fear. I can't let it kill me.

They made it to the bottom and Trina began walking through the space, moving her free hand in strange little circles as though she were stirring the air with it.

He shared a brief glance with Jeremiah and could tell that the other man thought she was just as weird as Mark did. It was small comfort. The worst part of all of this was it had been his idea to come here. There was something he had wanted to look for, but now all he could think about was getting out and he couldn't even remember why they had come down there.

Suddenly Trina twisted on her heel and marched straight for the back wall. She put her hand on it.

"There's something back here," she said.

He nodded numbly. That seemed right. Something about hidden rooms and something Cindy was allergic to.

He and Jeremiah rushed forward, more to stay close to the light from the flashlight than to actually see what she'd found. "What is it?" he asked, hating the fact that he could hear his voice shake. Excess adrenalin, that was all that was. His body's fight or flight response was in high gear.

"A room, I think. Something. Help me look for a way to open the wall," Trina said.

The three of them spread out and began systematically examining the wall, pressing on every stone, looking for telltale indentations. After twenty minutes they still hadn't found anything and he could tell the others were getting as frustrated as he was.

Suddenly Trina made a little exclamation and slammed her hand flat against the wall hard.

The earth beneath Mark felt like it moved and he staggered, struggling to catch his balance. Trina was saying something, but she was speaking so softly he couldn't make out her words. Suddenly part of the wall moved, swinging open on silent hinges. And just like that all the fear he'd been feeling intensified.

Something was very wrong, but before he could decide what to do about it his phone rang. He yanked it out of his pocket and saw that it was an unknown number. He was about to put it away when something urged him to answer.

"Hello?" he asked, his voice echoing around the basement.

He heard heavy breathing on the other line. It didn't sound like an obscene phone call, though. It sounded like someone was terrified and out of breath.

"Hello, who is this?"

"Mark," a tiny voice squeaked into the phone.

Shock surged through him as he recognized it. "Lizzie, where are you?"

"Help me," she whispered. "She was distracted, but she'll be-"

He heard a muffled sound and the line went dead.

13

"Lizzie? Lizzie!" Mark shouted as the call ended and then slammed his fist into the wall hard enough to hurt, but not hard enough to break bone.

"That was her?" Jeremiah asked.

"Yes, she asked for help. She said 'she was distracted, but she'll be' and then the call was cut off."

"We tripped the witch's intrusion alarms pulling focus long enough for Lizzie to get to a phone. Let's keep going and see what other chaos we can cause," Trina said.

Mark didn't want to keep going. He wanted to scream in frustration, but that wouldn't help him get his sister-in-law back. He also wanted to run out of that house and never come back, but that wouldn't help him find the killer who'd already sacrificed two young women. He forced himself to take a deep breath and then he followed Trina into the hidden room.

There was a large trunk in one corner and what looked like an altar in another one. There was a chair, what looked like some kind of metal cauldron, and a table with bunches of different looking herbs. He was so keyed up that he felt like he was seeing everything with a kind of hyper clarity and he knew that he wasn't doing well because he was almost disappointed that there were no skulls or jars labeled 'Bat's Wing' or 'Eye of Newt'.

Inside the cauldron on the floor was what smelled like charcoal with some type of crushed leaves, or rather, what was left of them.

"What's in here?" he asked.

Trina glanced at it. "Acacia leaves."

"Cindy was right," Mark said.

"This must have been burning while we were down here on Monday," Jeremiah said quickly.

"Which means our killer could have been here, too, watching us, laughing, seeing how badly she could scare us," Mark ground out through his teeth. Maybe that was the voice he'd heard. Not some mystical, otherworldly thing, but someone in here, watching, mocking. He was furious at how easily he'd been taken in by the dog and pony show. That was, until he remembered that two girls were dead and with nothing to link either of them to their murderer. Whatever was happening in here, it wasn't amateur hour.

Behind him he swore for just a moment that he heard laughter, high-pitched and mocking. He turned around even though he didn't want to, but it was just the three of them.

"Did anyone else hear that?" he asked sheepishly.

Jeremiah shook his head, but Trina looked at him sharply. "What did you hear?" she demanded, voice low and intense.

"Laughter."

"Stay close," she said.

He wanted to laugh himself. Where did she think he was going to go? It was getting hotter. He could feel sweat rolling down his back now. With each second that passed he wished himself far away from this place.

Pine Springs was just close enough to Los Angeles that they had a high-end costume shop in town, one that specialized in both original costumes and even rented and sold costumes that had been used by different movie houses. It was not a cheap place which was why Cindy was surprised to find herself roaming its aisles on her lunch break.

Geanie had brought her there and together they were ogling some of the famous pieces in the collection. Finally Cindy turned to Geanie. "Why are we here? I thought you and Joseph already had your costumes settled?"

"We do, silly. We're here to pick out a costume for you."

"Oh! There's no way I could spend this kind of money on a costume," Cindy said.

Geanie walked over and took her arm and rolled her eyes. "Who said anything about you spending your money?"

"Oh, I couldn't let you-"

"Of course you can. It's my party and I want our best friend to look perfect and have the most fantastic costume she can. What's the point of having money if you can't occasionally buy stuff for the people you love?"

"That's really sweet," Cindy said, feeling a warm glow. "It's nice to have best friends," she admitted.

Geanie smiled at her. "You haven't done nearly enough living, but we plan to change that."

Cindy smiled back. "So, as my benefactor, what costume did you have in mind?"

"Oh, I already picked it out. I was just enjoying browsing," Geanie said mischievously.

"Oh! And what exactly am I going to be dressed as?"

Geanie led the way over to a dressing room that had a beautiful old Spanish style gown hanging on it that looked like something from the Mission days. Cindy stared at it for a moment. The dress was beautiful, and hauntingly familiar.

"That looks like one of Elena de la Vega's dresses from The Mask of Zorro," Cindy said, sucking in her breath.

"I was hoping you'd recognize it!" Geanie said gleefully.

"You are kidding me!"

"Nope! All that's left for you is to try it on."

"There's no way it will fit me."

"I and the in-house tailor beg to differ. Now, go try it on."

Cindy went in the dressing room and tried the dress on with hands that shook slightly with excitement. She couldn't believe a dress she'd admired on screen was actually in her hands. When she slipped it on she was stunned to discover that it actually fit her pretty well. When she walked outside to model it Geanie clapped her hands with delight.

"The perfect Spanish señorita!"

"It's a little loose up top."

"We can have that fixed. I'm sure the tailor could take care of that in no time."

"Actually I think a safety pin or two would do it."

"If you want, sure. It does look stunning on you. I'm so glad I found this."

Cindy gingerly hugged Geanie then pulled back. "I have to admit, I'm afraid to hurt the dress. It must cost a fortune."

"I don't remember. I bought it last night."

Cindy gaped at her and Geanie shrugged. "I know you love the movie and when I discovered they had it, how could I not?"

The gentleman who had been behind the register when they came in walked over. He smiled at them both. "You were right, she looks stunning in it," he told Geanie.

Cindy felt herself blushing. Stunning was a word she was not used to having applied to her. She went back into the dressing room and changed into her regular clothes. A couple minutes later they were exiting the store with an enormous garment bag that it was taking both of them to carry.

Once they had settled in Geanie's car Cindy glanced at the clock. "Just enough time to grab some drive through burgers and make it back to our desks," she noted.

"On our way," Geanie said, putting the car in reverse.

Suddenly a wave of terror rolled over Cindy, startling her and making her gasp out loud.

"What's wrong?"

"I don't know, but something is happening," Cindy ground out. She could feel it. Someone was in terrible danger. She didn't know how she knew, she just did. Her thoughts flew to Jeremiah and as terror took hold of her she began to pray.

They had been searching the basement and going over the items in the hidden room for a couple of minutes and with each moment that had ticked by Mark's skin had been crawling more and more. He wanted out of there.

"These things have been in here a while," Trina noted. "I don't think this house was chosen at random. I think whoever is behind this has been planning things for a while, biding their time. This feels more like a headquarters than anything else."

"But the place is abandoned. There's nothing upstairs," Mark said.

"Did you actually go upstairs yourself, Detective?" she asked.

"Not myself, no," he admitted.

"Then you don't know for sure what's up there, only what other people thought they saw or didn't see. And as we know from our discovery of this room, the looks of this place can be deceiving," she noted.

Mark didn't know what to think. "Okay, then I'll tell you what. The three of us can tear this place apart from top to bottom and see what else we find."

Why am I saying that? he wondered. He must be going crazy. The only thing he should have been saying was a plea for them all to get the heck out of there. He started to turn, realizing that at least searching upstairs meant getting out of the basement. Something gleaming caught his eye.

On a small table in the corner that he had thought was empty there was a small piece of glass. There was something odd about it though. It reflected light almost more like some sort of gemstone or crystal. He felt drawn to it. He took a step. Another. He reached out his hand to pick it up.

Something sharp pricked his finger. With an exclamation he pulled his hand back.

"What is it?" Trina asked sharply.

"Nothing, I just cut my finger," Mark said.

"On what?" Jeremiah asked.

Jeremiah sounded far away, though, muted.

Something hard slammed into Mark's head and it took him a moment to realize it was the stone floor. He must have fallen.

"Mark!" he heard Jeremiah shout his name.

Something was deeply wrong. He could feel it. In one stunned moment he realized that Traci had been right. This house was going to kill him.

"I don't know what's wrong with him!" Trina shouted as she bent over Mark's body.

Jeremiah's eyes were fixed on Mark's index finger which had blood on it. "He's been poisoned," he said.

And given how fast it was acting they only had seconds before he was going to die.

14

"Call 911!" Jeremiah shouted as he yanked his belt off and wrapped it around Mark's upper arm up by the armpit. It was probably already too late, but he had to try. He yanked the flashlight out of Trina's hand and she gave a startled yelp even as she was dialing her phone with the other hand.

He unscrewed the flashlight and as the light flickered off the compartment opened. He grabbed one of the batteries out of it, a C size by the feel of it. He put the battery under Mark's armpit against the artery there and the nerve cluster just behind it. He clamped the belt down hard over the battery, driving it deep into Mark's armpit and he tightened it down as hard as he could. Even though Mark was slipping into unconsciousness he groaned in agony. Jeremiah knew the pain had to be excruciating.

"Officer down, he's been poisoned," Trina was saying into the phone. She gave the address.

"It's probably a neurological poison," Jeremiah barked and she repeated it into the phone.

That was what would explain just how fast it had started to react. All he could hope to do was cut off the flow of blood up Mark's arm, even reverse it as best he could. By applying the pressure of the battery where he did and holding it in place with the belt it not only acted like a tourniquet but it also put pressure on the nerve cluster which would slow down the transmission of the poison through his nervous system.

"What can I do?" Trina asked once she was off the phone.

"Pray, and see what you can figure out about the poison without getting it in your own system. Does it have a color, odor? Gather all the information you can quickly for the EMTs."

She clicked on the flashlight app on her phone and headed to the table where Mark had cut himself. Jeremiah continued to keep the pressure up, doing everything he could, and praying frantically. He had not gained a brother just to lose him.

A minute later Trina was back at his side, kneeling next to him and Mark. Her hand hovered over Mark's forehead. "I don't know how to help, what to do," she said, her voice agitated.

"Go upstairs and get the EMTs down here safely as soon as they arrive. Tell them everything you can so they're prepared when they get down here," he said.

She hesitated, still hovering.

"Go!" he thundered.

She scrambled to her feet and raced up the stairs, taking the light from her phone with her and plunging Mark and him into complete darkness. As her footsteps retreated they were left in utter blackness, cold and silent as a tomb. Jeremiah knew from experience that such complete sensory deprivation could lead to a number of problems ranging from anxiety to inability to properly judge the passage of time. Those could be a problem in any ordinary place, but they were deeply compounded when the darkness and silence was in a place already disturbing and filled with traumatic memories.

Even though he knew that they were alone in the basement, it didn't feel that way. It was as though a strange and terrible presence was there with them, pressing in around them with malevolent intent. The place was haunted, that was what his uncle would say. Sometimes the history and the memories inspired by a place could be as present as any phantom.

He did know that the darkness here was oppressive. Terrible things had happened here, and while it was not something he often gave great thought to he suspected that something demonic might be at play. Letting his thoughts linger on such things, though, would help neither of them.

"Mark, it's going to be okay. We're going to get through this," he said out loud, chasing the silence away. "You claimed me as family and if you think you're getting out of that so easy, you've got another thing coming."

On the one hand it was good that Mark was unconscious because otherwise the pain he would be experiencing would be unbearable and Jeremiah would likely have had to struggle with him to keep the battery and the belt in place. On the other hand it worried him because it would make it easier for Mark to slip away from him. If the other man was screaming at least he would know he was alive and fighting.

"You sure picked a heck of a time to investigate a crime scene without wearing some kind of protective gloves," Jeremiah said. Truth be told whatever had cut him probably would have sliced through the thin disposable gloves he knew Mark carried with him for when he had to handle evidence.

Something moved in the dark to his left and Jeremiah swung his head that direction. He couldn't see anything in the absolute blackness, but he had heard something. His heart began to beat faster as he considered the options. It was possible there was another way into this room from somewhere else in the house or even a tunnel to the outside. If that was the case the killer might be there with them. Whatever it was it had been too large to be a rat or a mouse.

He held his breath, straining to listen. After a moment there was movement again, a faint scratching sound accompanied by a dragging noise.

If the killer of that first girl had really been in this room while the police had investigated the house had he or she stayed until the police left hours later. Or was there really another way out?

Jeremiah shifted slightly, moving as silently as he could but positioning himself so he was facing the direction from which the sound was coming. It was one of the corners of the secret room. He tensed his muscles, preparing to defend himself and Mark and hoping that his adversary would be as blind as he was.

More scratching and dragging. Whatever it was it was getting closer. He had his phone in his pocket and he could reach for it and shine his light into the darkness. That would leave him vulnerable, though, even if just for a couple of seconds. It was no good calling Trina for help either since he didn't know her number.

He raised himself silently into a crouching position, preparing to lunge in any direction he needed to. He thought he heard for a moment the distant wail of a siren. Perhaps Trina and the EMTs would be down shortly. He had a feeling, though, it wouldn't be before whatever was creeping toward him in the darkness attacked. He waited, tense, ready, wishing he knew what kind of weapons the creature in the darkness had.

Or if what is over there is even human.

He tried to shake the thought from his mind. It was just this place making him panic, imagine things. Whatever was creeping toward him was alive and corporeal, not some ghost or demon.

Suddenly he heard a new sound. It was coming from upstairs. Trina must be on her way. Which meant that now was the time it should attack him if it was going to. He stayed still, waiting, refusing to leave Mark's side. He would let his enemy come to him.

Then he heard voices and a moment later footsteps on the stairs. Any moment now and light would fill the room and he'd see just what he was up against. If whatever was there was going to attack, it was now or never.

"We're coming!" he heard Trina call, voice frantic.

A sudden stab of light shot through the dark, and he winced against the brightness after so long in the darkness. He threw a hand into the air to shield his eyes from the light.

And he felt a needle jab him in the thigh.

Before he could react light suddenly flooded the room. Squinting he looked down and realized it wasn't a needle that had stabbed him, but a claw. A black cat had his paw on his leg and was shaking. The poor animal looked like it had been mangled, but it was still alive. He realized that's what he'd heard, the animal dragging its body across the floor to him from whatever hiding place it had been in.

"Can you move out of the way, sir," one of the EMTs said tersely.

Jeremiah carefully picked the cat up and it pressed itself close against his chest as he stood up. He moved over to Trina and she glanced at the cat. "Where did he come from?"

"Somewhere in this room. That corner over there, I think," he said, pointing.

"But we searched this place."

"Apparently he found a hiding place we didn't. It's probably what saved his life."

Her eyes drifted over to where the EMTs were working on Mark. "He looks in rough shape."

"They both are," he said, not sure if she was referring to Mark or the cat.

A short while later Jeremiah was happy to be standing outside in the sun, away from the house, as Mark was being loaded into the back of the ambulance on a stretcher. The men seemed to have gotten him stabilized and Jeremiah was starting to believe everything might be okay. He started to get in the back of the ambulance, but Trina stopped him with a hand on his arm.

"I still need help searching the rest of this house," she said.

He took a deep breath, barely holding back a harsh retort. She was right. There was nothing more he could do for Mark, but he could keep on the search for Lizzie and the killer.

"I know a good vet, I'll drop him off on the way to the hospital," the driver said, indicating the cat that Jeremiah was still holding.

"Let him know the cat is a potential witness to a homicide and any forensic evidence he can collect off him should be reported to the police," Trina said.

The man nodded and Jeremiah reluctantly surrendered the cat. The poor thing had probably been trapped in the house since before the murder and was likely in as desperate need of water as he was medical attention.

As the ambulance drove off he quickly called both Liam and Traci to let them know that Mark had been poisoned and was on his way to the hospital. He was about to call Cindy as well, but decided to wait until he had left the crime scene. She wouldn't take kindly to him continuing to look around the place where Mark had been poisoned. Better to tell her everything afterward.

A couple hours later Jeremiah and Trina staggered outside the house, sweaty and disheveled. Upstairs they had found one bedroom that was clearly being occupied and Jeremiah had no idea how Mark's people had missed that. They'd found another hidden room upstairs that was reached through a linen closet. There hadn't been much of interest inside it, though. They'd also found a tiny hole in the wall in the hidden room downstairs that the cat had likely secreted himself in, hiding from his attacker. It had been hard to see with the way it was blocked from view by the trunk that occupied the one wall.

He checked his phone and found that he had a missed call from Cindy, wanting to check in with him, and another from Traci letting him know that the doctor had said that Mark was going to be okay, thanks to his efforts.

He relayed the information to Trina who looked relieved. "I'll follow up on the cat, see what more we can find from him," she said.

Jeremiah wanted nothing more than to go home, take a hot shower, and go to bed. He glanced at his phone, though, and saw that he only had a few minutes before he was supposed to be teaching the scare class at the church. He'd been a fool to agree to do it, especially with everything that was going on. He should call and cancel, but Wildman would just try and get him to come out on Sunday. After all, what was happening with the murder investigation didn't involve Wildman or the kids or their haunted house.

Jeremiah made it back to the church with five minutes to spare. He took a moment to himself in the car to mentally prepare. Dealing with kids was always unpredictable and you had to be ready to roll with the punches. Sometimes literally. Wildman hadn't said how many kids he was expecting to show up to the workshop. Given that it was a weeknight, he figured the number would be fairly small.

Having taken a few quick cleansing breaths he got out of his car and walked to the gym. His jaw dropped when he got inside. There were at least thirty kids from high school and college sitting on the bleachers. When he walked toward the front where a microphone had been set up and Wildman was standing they all began to cheer.

One of the first things he noticed was that the entire front row was made up of familiar faces. Jeremiah's Rangers were all grinning at him, looking proud as could be. They were the kids who had followed him through the wilderness when they were attacked at Green Pastures camp.

Brenda and Sarah were sitting front and center, holding hands, mutually supporting each other. Both of them had clearly been crying for a very long time given the puffiness and redness around their eyes. They both managed to give him smiles, though. Flanking them on either side were the boys. Noah, Zac, Bobby, Stuart, Tray and Tim were all there along with the rest.

Half the kids in that room went to the synagogue, not the church. He'd no idea they'd signed up to help out the church with its haunted house. He felt a swell of pride. It had been a year-and-a-half since Green Pastures but he could see that they remembered. He could also see that all the other kids there who hadn't lived through what they had were looking at the kids in the front row with the same amount of awe and respect with which they were looking at him.

"I don't know what to say," Jeremiah said when he stepped up to the microphone.

"That's okay, Rabbi, we do," Zac shouted.

"Rangers! Rangers!" his kids started the chant and the rest picked it up. He turned to look at the pastor who was smiling at him.

"These kids love you, and they'll never forget what you did for them," Dave said. "You know that even though the ones you led through the wilderness came from different backgrounds, different religions, and were different ages each one of them has stayed fast friends with the others?"

"I had no idea," he admitted.

"You didn't just save them. You changed them. In some cases you even changed their families. Zac was on the verge of running away from home because he couldn't stand the screaming in his house while his parents were getting a divorce. You helped him go live with his grandparents and because of that and the changes they saw in him when he came back from Green Pastures it made them re-evaluate their own lives. They got marital counseling and reconciled. He moved back in with them just in time to spend his senior year at home."

Through Jeremiah's mind what Mark had told him in the pub came back. There were people here in Pine Springs who loved him and standing in front of those kids he had never felt so humbled in his entire life.

He cleared his throat and then took the microphone in his hand. "I just have one question. Who's ready to learn how to scare the pants off people?"

There was a thunderous chorus of "me" and all the kids jumped to their feet screaming.

"Okay," he said when they quieted down slightly. "Then let's get started."

Cindy had just finished eating dinner when she glanced at the clock on the microwave. It was six-thirty. Jeremiah should be teaching kids how to scare people. In a few minutes prayer chain members would arrive at the hospital to pray over Samuel. She hoped for his sake that it worked. She rinsed off her plate and put it in the dishwasher.

As she dried her hands she glanced at the clock again. She had enough time to get there if she wanted to go, too. The thought hadn't occurred to her until just then. She wasn't actually a member of the prayer chain, just the liaison between it and the church.

Suddenly, though, she felt an overwhelming urge to actually go and be a part of what they were doing tonight. She made a snap decision and five minutes later she was in the car on her way.

Once she got there she was relieved to see that there were indeed fifteen church members there. A woman in a dark suit who Cindy guessed to be the F.B.I. agent Mark had told them about nodded at her as she came into the room.

"Thank you so much for coming," the woman said, addressing the group. "My name is Trina, I work for the F.B.I. and I'm here investigating some serious crimes. This man could hold a key piece of information. His name is Samuel and he's been in a coma for nearly two years. I've called you together so that we might pray over him for his full and complete recovery."

Heads bobbed up and down around the room as people signaled their understanding. Trina moved over next to the hospital bed and placed her right hand on Samuel's forehead. She reached out with her left hand and the woman standing closest to her moved to take it. One by one they all linked up so they were standing in a circle around the bed. The man on the far end put his hand on Samuel's shoulder and everyone bowed their heads.

The little old lady who was holding Cindy's right hand began the prayer out loud. "Father, we bring before you this boy Samuel. He is ill, Lord, and only Your tender mercies can heal him. We, Your servants, come before You in prayer and supplication. We lift him up to You and we ask, heal him of whatever is wrong so that he might wake from this sleep that has stolen years of his young life."

She finished and someone on the other side of the circle began to pray. Cindy felt a tingling in her spine and a warmth flooding through her hands. Peace washed over her as she listened to the prayers around her and added her own silent pleas for healing and restoration. She was amazed at the power of the prayers and regretted that she had never joined with this amazing group before in lifting someone up in prayer.

When a moment of silence came she finally had the courage to speak up herself. "God, please heal Samuel now, tonight."

That was all she had to say. It wasn't long or eloquent like many of the others, but it was from her heart. Around the circle others kept on praying. The longer they prayed the more warmth seemed to infuse her until she felt drowsy. Her legs were beginning to feel rubbery, like the energy was leaving them. Finally the last person prayed and ended it with a strong 'Amen' which they all chorused.

They all looked up, still in a circle, still holding hands. They stared at Samuel, who was so still in his hospital bed. His cheeks were flushed and she didn't remember them being that way earlier.

Then, suddenly, Samuel's eyes flew open.

15

Cindy gasped along with everyone else.

From his hospital bed Samuel looked up at all of them, eyes wide and uncomprehending. Trina smiled and patted him on the shoulder. "Welcome back to the land of the living," she said.

He struggled to move his mouth like he wanted to say something.

"Take it easy," she warned. "You've been through a lot."

Seconds later doctors and nurses were pouring into the room, looks of shock on all their faces.

Cindy stepped back and marveled at what had just happened. She was beyond exhausted and she was sure that once she went to bed she'd sleep for a week, but she felt a glow, an excitement. It had worked! They had managed to bring this guy out of his coma. She was so grateful that she had made the last minute decision to come and be a part of it all. It would have been so hard to believe if she hadn't seen it with her own eyes.

She felt tears welling in her eyes and she marveled at the miracle before her.

"Everyone, can we clear this room for just a few minutes?" one of the doctors was saying.

Cindy shuffled out into the hallway with the others. There several people leaned against walls or sat down on the floor. They all looked like she felt - elated but drained.

Trina approached Cindy. "Thank you. This wouldn't have been possible without your help," she said.

"I was just glad we could get people out here," Cindy told her. "If we'd known about him, about his condition, maybe we could have helped sooner."

"Maybe. Or maybe it was just perfect timing and now was the time he was meant to be healed," Trina said. "Honestly, though, I'm overwhelmed by the outpouring of faith and compassion. First Shepherd must be one special place."

"We like to think so," Cindy said with a smile. "Although at the end of the day we're just a church like any other, struggling to get through and discover God's will for our lives and live every day to the best of our abilities."

"The faith you all displayed was still quite remarkable."

"Thank you. And thank you for suggesting we come out to pray."

"I'd love to tell you it was altruistic, but it was purely selfish on my part. I believe that guy in there can help us solve this whole mystery. But he couldn't do that from his coma."

"I hope you're right," Cindy said fervently. "This can't go on much longer. I keep thinking it's only a matter of time before the next body shows up."

"I'm afraid you're right. In my experience, there always is a next body."

Cindy shuddered "I'm glad I don't have your job."

Trina smiled. "I understand. There are days I wish I didn't have my job. But then there are days where everything comes together and I can help save lives and initiate healing for those who have lost something."

"That will be good. There's a lot of healing that needs to go on here in Pine Springs."

"What makes you say that?"

Cindy thought of Jeremiah and all he'd been through, and the trauma that Traci and her sisters were suffering. She opened her mouth, but then quickly closed it again. "I'm sorry, it's not my place to really say. I can't believe I've said as much to you as I have. You're very easy to talk to."

Trina smiled. "I get that a lot. Remember, though, if you do need to talk, I'm always ready to listen."

"Thanks, I'll keep that in mind," Cindy said. "Right now, though, I'm planning on getting some sleep."

"You've earned it. Have pleasant dreams tonight," Trina said.

"Thanks," Cindy said, feeling warm and fuzzy inside. "I think I just might."

Jeremiah was well into his second hour with the kids and they were just as enthusiastic as they had been at the beginning. He had taught them ways to jump out and surprise people, noises to make that would pray on people's base instincts, and what type of noisemakers and props to use to engender terror in their victims. Now, though was the ultimate lesson.

"Are you ready to learn your secret weapon?" he asked them.

Kids jumped up and down, roaring approval and willingness to learn.

"Okay, for this I need three volunteers."

Hands shot up all over the room. This time he was careful to choose kids who did not know him. He had three of them line up in front of the others with their backs to him. "Okay, now I want each of you to silently count to ten in your head when I say go. When you hit ten, turn around. Okay, begin."

He noticed that a couple of the kids were bobbing their heads up and down with their counting. He barely managed to hold back a chuckle as he crept up silently behind the biggest of the guys. He positioned himself so that he was directly behind the guy and waited for him to finish the ten count. A couple seconds later the kids began turning around. When the guy he was standing behind turned he found himself face-to-face with Jeremiah with only a mere inch between them. He shouted and leaped backward before losing his balance and landing on his rump. The kids next to him scattered, screaming as well.

Applause broke out around the room as Jeremiah helped him back to his feet. Then he returned to the microphone. "Silence, is the most frightening thing of all," he explained. "People are waiting for the jump moments, the screams, the music crescendos. What they can't prepare for is what they don't see or hear coming. The silence gets them every time. Sure, they might run if a zombie is chasing them through the maze, but if you want to cause the most terror the way to do it is to move silently and don't draw attention to yourself until you want to be seen."

He pulled a couple more volunteers up out of the audience. "Let me show you one way to do this particularly well."

He pointed to the guy. "Now, you're walking through the maze and you're still looking behind you because there was a particularly loud, obnoxious monster behind you and you want to make sure he's not following you. So, walk while looking backward."

The guy did as he was instructed. Jeremiah took the girl and walked her next to the guy, but with her hand extended mere inches in front of his head.

"And turn around," Jeremiah instructed.

The guy turned around and saw the girl's hand two inches from his face and he shrieked and backpedalled.

"The unexpected. Gets them every time," Jeremiah said as the crowd roared its approval. He handed the microphone back to Dave and the pastor beamed at him.

"Thank you, Rabbi Silverman, for coming out and teaching us how to be scarier than we already are."

Everyone laughed at that, too.

"Now remember, we have an all day workday Sunday after church to finish getting the maze put together. Remind everyone about it and bring some work clothes to change into after church. We will be providing pizza and soda for everyone who comes help build."

That news was met by more wild applause. Dave winked at him. "You got them really wound up, great job. Now comes the fun part. We get to send them home to their parents this hyper."

When Mark woke it took him a few moments to figure out where he was. Slowly he realized he was in a hospital bed. He turned his head and saw Traci sitting in a chair nearby, head bowed and hands folded.

"Hey," he said, his voice sounding gravelly.

Her head jerked up and she gave out a cry of relief. She lunged forward and hugged him. "I was so scared," she whispered against his cheek.

"It's going to be okay," he said managing to lift his hand and pat her shoulder. "What happened?"

"Jeremiah called, said you'd been poisoned and that an ambulance was taking you here. The doctor said that whatever Jeremiah had done to stop the spread of the poison saved your life. He said that you need to rest for a couple of days but you should be okay."

Mark nodded. He would have to thank Jeremiah.

"So, how was your day?" he asked.

She gave him a short, harsh laugh and stroked his hair. "I got you a Dick Tracy costume, myself a Tess Trueheart costume and little gangster costumes for the children."

"They'll be adorable," he assured her.

She slowly sat back down next to him, but continued to hold onto his arm. Her eyes were puffy and he could tell she'd been crying.

"How long was I out?" he asked.

"Six hours I think. The worst six hours of my life."

Given some of the things they'd been through, that was saying a lot.

"Did Jeremiah and Trina find anything else in the house?" he asked.

"What house?"

"The one where we found the first victim."

165

Suddenly Traci went very still. "That's where you were when you were poisoned?" she asked, pulling her hand away from his arm.

"Yeah. We found this secret room in the basement. On this table I saw a bit of mirror that looked almost more like a crystal. I went to pick it up and the next thing I know I'm on the floor."

"You went back there after you promised me that you wouldn't?"

"I'm sorry. It couldn't be helped. I had to find out if something was missed the other day, and it was."

"*You* had to find out? It sounds like Jeremiah and Trina were there."

He nodded. "Trina found the secret room."

"So, you didn't have to be there. The F.B.I. was handling it. You went, knowing what I felt, knowing that I thought something terrible was going to happen to you there."

He looked into her eyes and suddenly realized that he was in trouble. He had never seen her so angry. "I'm sorry."

"Sorry? You're sorry? For which part? Ignoring me and my instincts, nearly getting yourself killed in the process, or getting caught?" She stood up and she was shaking from head to toe. "You purposely endangered your life."

"A cop needed to go."

"That's bull and you know it. The F.B.I. was there and last I checked, they trump you. And if it was so important a cop go, you could have asked Liam to go. No, instead you had to go and risk your life after I told you I didn't want you back there."

"It's my job-"

"And there it is. Your job is more important than your family, than me. Listen, Mark. I've put up with a lot of crap because of your job, but I will not put up with this. I have Rachel and Ryan to think about now. It's bad enough that you don't care enough about me to do the right thing, but you don't care enough about them. I can't live like this. I won't live like this."

Mark was stunned. "What are you saying?"

"I'm saying we're done."

He felt his heart stutter and his chest tightened painfully. He struggled to sit up. He reached for her hand, but she snatched it away. "Traci, please, we've been through worse than this. I'm fine."

"You and I have been through worse than this, yes, and I was willing to do it while it was you and I. I have the children to think about now, and I won't put them through the same horror I go through, sitting up at night, wondering if you're going to make it home or if you're lying dead somewhere. I won't put my children through that terror."

"Traci, you're upset, I understand, but you don't mean what you're saying," he choked out.

"Did you even think about what I'd said, about promising me you'd stay away from that house when you went in it?" she asked.

"Every step," he admitted.

She shook her head. "The sad part is, I'm not sure if that makes what you did better...or worse."

"Look, I'm sorry, I'll never do something so stupid again."

"You and I both know that's a lie."

"I'll quit my job."

"And do what? It's in your blood, and you'd only resent me and the kids for making you give it up. I'm done talking."

Tears had started to spill down her face. She picked up her jacket, turned and marched out the door.

"Wait!" Mark shouted.

He struggled to sit up the rest of the way. He swung his legs over the edge of the bed, tried to stand, and ended up collapsed on the floor. He could hear one of the infernal monitors they had him hooked up to change its beeping pattern. As he struggled to get back up the door flew open and a nurse rushed in. Once she saw him her expression changed and she shook her head.

"You need to stay in bed for the next couple of days. As you see, you're too weak to get up by yourself."

"I have to. It's a matter of life and death."

"Oh no, I've heard every excuse you can think of buddy, and that won't cut it."

She leaned down and put her arms around him. "Let's get you back up on the bed."

"Help me out of here."

"No."

"I'm a cop."

"You're a sick cop."

"I could shoot you," he said, desperate.

"With what gun? Your partner took charge of that a while back."

She got him back up on the bed and he collapsed, not even able to hold himself upright.

"At least get me my phone."

"That I will do if you say the magic word."

He had never hit a woman, but he was on the verge of doing so now. "Please," he said through gritted teeth.

"That's better."

She went to the closet and a moment later returned, handing him his phone. He called Traci, but it just went to voicemail. He tried three more times but it did the same. She must have turned her phone off. Finally he left a message. It was garbled, incoherent. He realized halfway through it that he was crying, but he forced himself to keep talking. The battery on his phone beeped and then gave out before he did.

With a scream of anguish he fell backward.

16

When the doctor and nurses emerged from the room where Samuel was most of the prayer group had left, but Cindy was still there along with Trina. She felt warm and happy and exhausted, but she wanted to actually hear what the doctor said before she went home. It was the first time she'd been able to participate in anything quite like this and she wasn't ready for the experience to end.

When the medical staff did emerge they all looked amazed. The doctor smiled at Cindy and Trina. "I'm calling it. It's a miracle," he said. "I've never seen anything quite like that."

"When will I be able to speak with him?" Trina asked.

"Ordinarily I'd say wait until tomorrow and let him rest tonight, but I think he's done quite enough of that. So, feel free to go in."

"Thank you," Trina said.

The doctor nodded and walked off, looking at the chart and shaking his head.

"I'm glad you're going to hopefully get some answers. Are you going to call Mark?" Cindy asked.

Trina shook her head. "I'm not sure he's up to it yet. Although I will swing by his room and pop my head in after I'm done. See how he is."

"His room?" Cindy asked, confused.

"Yes. Sorry, I assumed you knew. He was poisoned earlier today and he should be here in the hospital."

"Poisoned?" Cindy said, feeling like she'd been punched in the stomach.

Trina nodded. "Jeremiah saved his life. That rabbi is quite the hero."

Cindy nodded stiffly, wondering why this was the first she was hearing of any of this. "Do you know what room Mark's in?" she asked.

"No, but I'm sure the nurse's station can tell you," Trina said. She smiled. "Wish me luck."

"Good luck," Cindy said as she watched Trina walk back into Samuel's room. As soon as the door had closed she turned on her heel and made her way to the nearest nurse's station, feeling like she was in a fog. She'd known earlier that something was wrong. Why hadn't she called Jeremiah? What was it Mark had said? The three of them needed to get their mojo back. Boy was he not kidding.

One of the nurses was able to point her in the direction of Mark's room. When she walked in he started up. "Traci?" His face fell. "Hi, Cindy," he said, collapsing back against his pillows.

She had never seen anyone look so pale and it scared her. She'd thought he was going to be okay, but looking at him she wasn't so sure. "Mark, are you okay?" she asked, her voice coming out as little more than a papery whisper.

"No, I'm not," he said, his voice breaking.

Fear wrapped around her heart and squeezed. She rushed over next to him and grabbed his hand. "I'm sure you're going to be fine," she said, hating that she could hear the tremble in her voice.

"No, I won't be, and there's no getting around that," he said, his eyes so full of grief that the tears started pouring down her cheeks. She still felt somewhat drained from the prayer session and her legs turned to rubber. She was going to collapse if she didn't sit.

She reached for the chair closest to her with her free hand and managed to yank it close just as she fell into it. "Oh, Mark, I'm so sorry," she said.

"I never dreamed this would happen. Not now. Not like this. Not after surviving so much," he said. "And I'm just stuck here in this bed. I can't even get up and do anything to fix this."

"Of course you can't," she told him, struggling to overcome her own emotions. He needed her strength, now more than ever. And Traci was going to need it once the end had come.

"Where, where is Traci?" she managed to ask, her heart breaking for her.

"I don't know," he said, tears shimmering in his eyes. "She's not answering her phone."

"Does she know?"

He looked at her like she had lost her mind. "Of course she knows. She's the one who told me."

The horror of that was nearly too much. To have to hear that he was dying from his wife instead of the doctor. She couldn't believe what that must have done to both of them.

"Does Jeremiah know?" she asked. Trina certainly didn't seem to. She had thought Mark was going to be okay.

"No. No one else knows but you," he whispered.

"What can I do for you?" she asked.

DEBBIE VIGUIÉ

"You have to help me get out of here. The nurses won't let me leave, and I can't stand up on my own. I tried earlier and just collapsed on the floor. My legs won't hold me up. I can barely sit up, but I can't be here. I can't just lie in this hospital bed while everything slips away from me."

"Where do you want me to take you?" she asked.

"Home first. Then, I don't know."

She nodded. She could do this for Mark. She owed him this much. She forced herself to her feet. "I'll find a wheelchair and then we'll get out of here."

"Thank you," he said, gripping her hand hard. "You are a true friend and I will never forget this."

She nodded and turned away, barely making it out into the hallway. She didn't want to sob in front of him. She leaned against the wall for a moment, trying to gather her wits about her. Then she headed for the elevator. She knew from experience that they kept wheelchairs ready and waiting at the entrance to the emergency room.

She pulled out her phone and called Jeremiah. Mark needed her and she needed him.

"Hello?" he answered.

"Where are you?" she asked.

"At home. I just got here a few minutes ago. I was teaching the kids at the church how to scare people for the haunted house."

"I'm at the hospital and I need you."

"Why, what's wrong?"

She took a deep breath. "Mark's dying."

"What!"

"Yes. He said you didn't know. He's asked me to get him out of here because he doesn't want...doesn't want to

173

die in here. I'm going to get a wheelchair and try to sneak him past the nurse's station. He wants to go home."

"I'll be there as fast as I can."

"Thank you," she whispered before hanging up.

Jeremiah was out the door and in the car in seconds. He didn't know what had happened. Mark had seemed stable when the EMTs had taken him away and he'd heard that the doctor at the hospital had said he was going to be okay. Maybe they'd misjudged the type of poison or the dosage.

He felt sick to the bottom of his soul. He had seen so much death in his life, lost friends to it, but he realized he'd never had a friend as close as Mark. Proverbs 18:24 spoke of a friend that was closer than a brother. It was a Proverb he had only just recently come to understand and he kept reciting it in his mind as he blew through three stop signs and two red lights.

He skidded into a parking slot at the hospital and raced inside. Cindy hadn't said where they were in the hospital. Before he could move the door to the nearest elevator opened and she emerged, pushing Mark in a wheelchair.

She moved quickly and Jeremiah fell into step beside them, leading them out to his car. Mark was ashen and Jeremiah felt his stomach knot more. "I'm so sorry," he whispered.

"It's not your fault," Mark said, his breathing ragged.

Jeremiah opened the door to the backseat of the car.

"Help me stand," Mark whispered.

Jeremiah shook his head. "I've got you." He put an arm under Mark's legs and another behind his back and picked him up. Cindy moved the wheelchair out of the way and

Jeremiah gently sat Mark down in the backseat. He closed the door and ran around to the driver's side as Cindy got in the passenger front seat.

Seconds later they were leaving the parking lot and heading for Mark's house.

He took one hand off the wheel and reached over to grab Cindy's hand, needing to feel her warmth. Tears began spilling down her cheeks, but she didn't say anything, just squeezed his hand back.

He wanted to say something, but words were failing him. Mark had slumped over sideways in the back seat. Jeremiah kept glancing in the rearview mirror every few seconds just to make sure that he was still alive.

Finally they pulled up in front of Mark's house. The lights were on inside and he hoped that Traci was there. He didn't know why she hadn't been at the hospital when they were breaking Mark out.

He parked in the driveway and was out of the car in a moment, going around to the back. Cindy raced up to the door with Mark's keys in her hand. Jeremiah moved around to the back of the car and lifted Mark out.

"I feel so helpless," Mark said.

"Don't worry about it," Jeremiah said softly.

Cindy pushed open the door just as they got there and he carried Mark inside and then set him down on the couch. Cindy closed the door.

"Traci!" she called, her voice cracking.

There was no answer.

"She's not here," Mark said, voice shaking.

"We'll find her," Jeremiah promised him.

"What if I never see her again?" Mark asked him with haunted eyes.

175

Jeremiah crouched down next to him so he could look him in the eyes. "I promise you, that's not going to happen."

Cindy was walking into the back of the house. She was back a minute later. "No one's here."

"Not even Buster," Jeremiah frowned as he realized that Mark's beagle wasn't there to greet them.

"She took them all with her," Mark said, his words somewhat slurred. His head was bobbing a bit. He was getting weaker.

"Where, where would she have taken Buster and the kids?" Jeremiah asked.

"I don't know. Maybe her sister's place."

"Amber?" Cindy asked.

Mark nodded. Sweat was beading on his forehead. A phone rang and Cindy pulled it out of her purse. "Mark, it looks like Trina is calling your phone," she said. "Do you want to talk to her?"

Mark stretched out his hand, but then it fell. "I don't think I can," he whispered.

Jeremiah's throat constricted. Mark was fading fast.

Cindy passed the phone to Jeremiah and sat down on the couch next to Mark.

"Hello, this is Jeremiah speaking," he said, doing his best to answer with a steady voice.

"Where on earth is Mark?" Trina demanded. "I've got a bunch of doctors and nurses here breathing down my neck. Apparently they think some woman helped him escape the hospital."

"That was Cindy. He begged her for her help." Jeremiah turned away from Mark and Cindy and lowered his voice.

"They wouldn't let him leave and he wanted to die at home."

"What?"

"Yes. So, that's where we are."

"He's not dying," Trina said.

"That's what I thought, too, but apparently we were wrong."

There was a pause and he could hear Trina talking to someone else. A few moments later she was back. "He's not dying, but he is very sick and he's supposed to be recovering in the hospital for a few days."

Jeremiah blinked as a tiny ember of hope flared to life inside him. "He's not dying?"

"No."

"Then why does he think he is?"

"I don't know, maybe he was hallucinating or something. The bottom line is, you need to get him back here. There's all kinds of fluids and medications he's supposed to be taking."

"Understood."

He hung up and turned back to Cindy and Mark. He leaned down to look at Mark whose eyelids were half closed over eyes that looked glassy and dazed. "Mark, you're not dying."

"He's not?" Cindy asked, eyes wide.

Mark's head lolled forward. "Of course I'm not."

"What!" Cindy said, grabbing Mark's shoulders. "Then what were you talking about in the hospital?"

Mark's head snapped back and forth and Jeremiah pulled Cindy off him. Then he had to fight down the urge to shake the man himself. He managed to get himself under control and asked, "What's going on, Mark?"

He stared at both of them. "Traci. She left me."

17

An hour later they were back in Mark's room at the hospital. He was back in bed and hooked up to a variety of monitors and an IV. He was pretty out of it, but a little bit better than he had been at his house. Cindy was just grateful that between him being a cop and whatever Trina had said the hospital staff seemed to be willing to look the other way about his temporary disappearance.

She was still shocked, though, about his revelation about Traci. He really hadn't managed to tell them anything else. He'd passed out in the house and hadn't woken up again until he was back in the hospital. One thing was certain, the doctors were right to want to keep him bedridden for a couple of days until his system could fully recover. She was relieved that at least taking him out of the hospital didn't seem to have actually done more damage.

Cindy had planned to tell him what she had found out about Cheyenne's sister, Lacey, but she wasn't sure that he would even remember anything she had to say. Before she could try, the doctors finally shooed them all out declaring that Mark needed sleep at that point more than anything else.

In the hallway Trina stifled a yawn. "I'm guessing I'll see you all tomorrow?" she said.

"Probably here at some point," Jeremiah affirmed.

"Good."

She headed toward the elevator and a minute later Cindy and Jeremiah followed. In the parking lot he walked her to her car. When they got to it he pulled her into his arms and hugged her tight. She hugged him back, bone weary in a way she hadn't been in a long time and emotionally spent.

"I was so scared," she whispered.

"So was I."

"I've got to talk to Traci, figure out what's going on with her, but I just want to sleep."

"You could call her tomorrow."

It was tempting, but she knew she wasn't going to be able to sleep if she didn't at least try. She was worried about both of her friends and didn't like what was happening.

"They have to be able to work this out," she said.

"I hope so."

It wasn't exactly the reassurance she was looking for, but at this point she'd take what she could get.

"Okay. I'll see you tomorrow," she said.

He nodded as she pulled away. "If you do talk to Traci, you should let her know what happened today."

"About Mark trying to get home to find her?"

"Yes, but that wasn't what I was talking about. I don't know what happened between them earlier and I don't know if he had a chance to tell her that Lizzie called him."

"Lizzie called?" Cindy asked, feeling suddenly hopeful.

"Yes," Jeremiah said, his voice grave. "At least we know something now, even if it isn't good. She is being held against her will. She was able to get to a phone for a few seconds and indicated that a woman was involved before she got cut off. Trina seemed to think that since we were in the house we might have tripped some sort of intrusion alarm distracting the woman."

"Poor Lizzie. Poor Traci," Cindy muttered. "I didn't get a chance to tell everyone what I learned today. Brenda, one of our high school students, was at the church today, hysterical because she had just found out that one of her closest friends was Cheyenne, the first girl that was killed. She told us that Cheyenne had an older sister, Lacey, who was cruel and had hurt Cheyenne often. Brenda believed Lacey would have been capable of killing her."

A look of concern filled Jeremiah's eyes.

"What is it?" she asked.

"Sarah and Brenda, they were the two girls who I was responsible for at Green Pastures. They were at the church tonight for the scare class. They both looked like they had been crying, but they were supporting each other and putting on brave faces. Sara's younger sister, Meghan, is the one who ran away, but I had no idea Brenda had lost her friend."

"Those two girls have been through so much," Cindy said softly, feeling her own emotions deeply.

"They're going to be there on Sunday to help finish the construction. I promised the kids I'd come, too, make some suggestions. I'll try to talk to them both more then."

"That would be nice. I know all the kids who were with you love and respect you," Cindy said.

"So I've been finding out."

"That surprises you?"

"I guess I had assumed I would be just part of a terrible memory that they'd be trying to forget."

She shook her head. "You bring out the best in people, push them to achieve things they never dreamed possible. No one's going to forget that."

He ducked his eyes, but didn't say anything.

"I should go if I'm going to try and reach out to Traci tonight," Cindy said.

He waited until she was in her car and had started it before turning to walk toward his own. All Cindy wanted was to sleep, but she knew that she had to at least try to talk to Traci.

She pulled out her phone and called Traci's cell. She was surprised and relieved when the other woman picked up.

"Hello?"

"Hey, it's Cindy. Can we talk?"

There was a pause so long Cindy checked to see if the call had dropped. Finally Traci said, "Okay."

"Awesome. Where are you?"

"I'm at Amber's house."

"Give me the address and I'll meet you there."

"Actually I'm the only one here awake. Why don't I meet you at the Starbucks down the street?"

"Sure, just tell me where to go."

Half an hour later Cindy was parking outside the coffee shop. It was farther than she'd wanted to drive, but at least traffic had been light. She staggered inside and was relieved to see that Traci was there. She looked like a wreck, but she hoisted two cups off the table and Cindy walked over.

"I got you a hot chocolate with raspberry. That's what you drink here, right?" Traci asked.

"It is," Cindy admitted as she sat down.

The thought of face-planting on the table was almost overwhelming, but she managed to remain upright as Traci handed her the hot chocolate.

"How are you?" Cindy asked.

"I've been better," Traci said. "How are you?"

Cindy took a sip of her drink and then set it down. "I had one of the most stressful nights of my life," she admitted. "I found out that Mark was in the hospital and why. Then, when I made it to his room to see how he was doing I realized that he was in much worse shape than I had been led to believe."

Cindy looked up, purposely watching Traci's face. "I took one look at him and knew something was desperately wrong. That's when I found out that I'd been misinformed and that he was actually dying."

Traci jerked and the color drained from her face. "What?" she whispered.

"Yeah, and the nursing staff refused to let him go home to take care of things he needed to do. He was so weak he couldn't even stand on his own and when he had tried to get out of bed he had collapsed on the floor."

Traci's hand was pressed over her heart and she had a look of pure distress on her face.

"He begged me to get him out of there so that he didn't have to lie there as his life slipped through his fingers. I did manage to smuggle him out and Jeremiah had to carry him from the wheelchair to the car and then again into the house. We were about to start to look for you when we got a call from a very upset F.B.I. agent who was being grilled by the doctors about his disappearance. Meanwhile, he had collapsed entirely on the couch and was fading fast. Then, we heard the news that he wasn't dying. Turns out when he told me his life was over and that he wasn't okay and couldn't be fixed, I thought he was talking about the poison. It turns out he was talking about the fact that you walked out on him."

Cindy tried to say the last part without sounding accusatory, but she wasn't sure how well she succeeded. She picked up her drink and took another sip. She was gratified to see that Traci had at least been showing signs of concern during her story.

"What happened?" Traci asked.

"We had to take him back to the hospital. It was a good thing, too. He's going to pull through, but his body desperately needed to be confined to bed and to be taking certain fluids and medications. In convincing me to help him escape, which I did because I thought he was dying, he could have been gravely injured. And given that he did pass out before we could get him back to the hospital, he never had a chance to explain to us what happened."

Traci was gripping her coffee with white knuckles. "I couldn't take it anymore, almost losing him, wondering when he was going to finally get himself killed. I found out he was poisoned in that house and I had such a bad feeling when he told me about the first victim that I made him promise me he wouldn't go back into that house again. And he did, and he didn't even need to since Jeremiah and Trina seemed to manage just fine without him once he had to be taken away to the hospital. If he won't take care of himself, try to protect himself for me and the kids, what can I do? I can't put them through that uncertainty. It's bad enough I lived with it for years but they don't need to grow up that way."

"They wouldn't be the first children of a police officer," Cindy said.

"No, but they're *my* first children and I want better for them than a life of fear and uncertainty, particularly if their father isn't willing to do his part to keep himself safe."

"Mark doesn't intentionally put himself in harm's way."

"Maybe not, but he doesn't do what he could to avoid it either," Traci retorted. "I told him I had a terrible feeling that he was going to die in that house. He should have listened to me. He should have respected me and cared about me and the kids enough to at least do that."

"Sometimes guys are idiots," Cindy said, vaguely aware that it sounded like something Wildman had said to her.

"And what does that make the women who stick with them even against their better judgment?"

"Loving wives."

Tears glimmered in Traci's eyes. "I love Mark. I do. I'm just tired of living with this uncertainty. Knowing that he broke his promise to me, that he went back there, and it didn't even have to be him that did it."

Cindy could understand where Traci was coming from. She could feel the other woman's pain and heartbreak. But she had seen Mark's and she knew that he could never live without her.

"Mark would walk through fire for you," Cindy said softly.

Traci didn't respond.

"I don't know what he got a chance to tell you in the hospital, and he certainly was out of it later, but Jeremiah was able to fill me in on something that happened earlier today that you should know about."

"What?" Traci asked.

"While they were in the house Lizzie called Mark, just for a second. She is being held captive by someone, she mentioned a woman. Before she could say anything else the call was disconnected."

Traci let out a sob and Cindy reached across the table to grab her hand. "I know Mark will do everything in his power to find her."

"Of course he will. That's who he is."

Cindy didn't know what else to say so she just sat quietly and held Traci's hand while she cried. She couldn't help but reflect that it had been such a day of terrible lows, but then there had also been the one incredible mountain top experience when she had gotten to pray with those wonderful people and see a miracle happen.

They all needed a few more of those miracles. And suddenly she heard herself saying softly, "God, I lift up Traci, Lizzie, and Mark to You that You might protect them and guide them and bring them all back together safely."

That was it, just the one small sentence, and she hadn't even expected to be praying it out loud. Traci had gone very still and after Cindy was done she looked up at her.

"Thank you," Traci breathed.

Cindy just smiled and squeezed her hand.

Mark woke slowly in the morning, feeling like he was coming out of some hideous nightmare. When he finally opened his eyes and saw where he was, though, he realized that the day before hadn't been a dream. He shuddered as everything came flooding back.

There were a lot of memories that were ingrained in his mind, burned there, and he was sure they always would be. Others, especially later in the evening, were incredibly fuzzy and he actually wondered if a couple of them were real or hallucinations. He hadn't actually managed to convince Cindy and Jeremiah to take him home, had he?

Of all the things swimming in his head, though, one was crystal clear. He needed to get hold of Traci. His phone was on the table nearby, charging. He grabbed it and as he pulled it free of the charging cable it began to ring.

It wasn't Traci and for a moment he thought about not even answering. He did, though. "Hello?"

"Hello, I'm looking for Detective Walters," a woman said.

"Speaking."

"Oh, Detective, I'm so glad. My name is Martha and I work at the humane society. I helped you adopt your Beagle a while back during all of that craziness."

"I remember. What can I do for you?"

"Well, we've had...something happen here at the humane society. Something awful, actually. I called the police, but the one I spoke with really didn't seem to understand the urgency of the situation. And I remembered you were an animal lover and you worked on that case with the dogs of the homeless being kidnapped, so I decided to take a chance and call you."

"What exactly happened?" he asked.

"Someone broke in last night and they stole several animals."

"That's terrible. Any chance that someone just really wanted a couple of dogs and didn't want to go through channels?"

"No chance, I'm afraid," she said her voice distressed. "I'm convinced that there is a terrible, sinister reason behind the kidnappings."

"Why?"

"They only stole the black cats."

18

"Black cats?" Mark asked, sitting up abruptly.

"Yes, and I'm afraid that I don't have to tell you, Detective, that there are a lot of sick people out there. We won't even adopt out black cats during the month of October. We're all so very worried for their safety."

"You were right to call," he said, his mind racing. "I'm going to send my partner, Liam, down there with a forensics team. Please, try to keep people away from the crime scene as much as possible. They're going to try and get fingerprints, that kind of thing."

"Bless you, Detective," Martha said, sounding like she was about to cry. "I'll do that."

He hung up and called Liam. Fortunately his partner picked up right away.

"Liam, you're on. I'm laid up in the hospital for at least a day or two."

"What happened?"

"I'll tell you later. Right now I need you to grab some forensic guys and get down to the humane society right away. Last night someone broke in and kidnapped their black cats and I think whoever did so could be linked to whoever's killing these girls and has kidnapped Lizzie."

"We know for sure that Lizzie's been kidnapped?"

"Yeah, like I said, I'll fill you in, but get down there now. Martha will be waiting for you."

"On it."

Next Mark checked the number that Lizzie had called in on yesterday. He cursed silently at all the time wasted because of his being poisoned. Next he called the precinct and was shortly connected with Daniels, an officer he'd used before when he needed someone with computer skills.

"Detective, what can I do for you?" the other man asked.

"I'm going to give you a phone number. I need it traced as part of a kidnapping case and I need it five minutes ago."

"Okay, go."

Mark rattled off the number and then hung up. He took a deep breath and tried calling Traci's number. It rang several times, but then went to voicemail.

"I love you, call me," he said and then hung up.

He leaned his head back. His mind was racing. There was so much to do and he couldn't believe that he was stuck there.

A few minutes later a nurse came in to check him over and another brought food which was terrible. He forced himself to scarf it down anyway. He wasn't going to convince anyone to let him out of this place if he didn't eat. While he was doing so Daniels called him with the disappointing news that Lizzie had called on a burner cell phone which had since been disabled. There was no way to track it. He hung up and went back to eating as he waited for more news.

He had just finished when the door opened and Trina walked in. "Looking better than yesterday, I see," she noted.

"Certainly feeling better."

"You're lucky to be alive. You wouldn't be if it wasn't for Jeremiah's quick thinking and obvious know-how."

"I'll be sure to thank him. Did you guys turn anything else up at the house?"

"Only thing of significance was a black cat that had been hiding in that hidden room. He was significantly the worse for wear. We got him to a veterinarian who was able to fix him up and check him over. He had a broken leg, several bruises, and was missing massive chunks of fur. He was also deeply dehydrated. Fortunately he's already on the mend and he was chipped so his owner will be able to retrieve him shortly."

"What was the cat's name?" Mark asked.

"Whiskers. Not terribly original."

"At least that's one kidnapped cat found," he said.

"One?"

"Yeah. Did they find anything on him?"

"There was human blood on his front paws and claws. They're trying to match it. Hopefully he scratched our killer. Now, what do you mean by one cat found?"

"Another cat from the same neighborhood that belonged to one of the wiccans was kidnapped around the same time as Whiskers. She was also a black cat. Then, the humane society was broken into last night and whoever did it stole their black cats. I've got my partner over there now looking into it."

"Sounds like I'm getting here at just the right time for the info dump," Jeremiah said, poking his head in the door.

"Yes, come in," Mark said with a wave of his hand.

The rabbi entered and took a seat. "So, there are more black cats out there that might be victimized by whoever attacked the one we found yesterday?"

"Yes," Mark said. "And the number Lizzie called in on yesterday was a burner phone that has almost certainly been dumped since then. Other than that, we've got nothing new."

"That's not entirely true," Trina said.

"Here either," Jeremiah answered.

"Okay, Trina you go then Jeremiah," Mark said, sitting up a little more and pushing his empty food tray farther from him.

"The prayer chain people gathered last night around Samuel and when it was all done he woke from his coma."

"Were you able to talk to him?" Mark asked eagerly.

"I was."

"And what did he say?"

"He said that Lizzie cursed him."

"He actually said that?" Mark asked, startled.

"Yes. Apparently they'd started having fights because he was afraid that her new coven was pulling her to the dark side. She wanted him to join, but he refused. He said that the people in it scared him and that they were into things that made him uncomfortable. He finally told Lizzie that if she didn't understand that, if she continued on the path that she was on, that he didn't think they could be together."

"I bet that went over well," Jeremiah said drily.

"Yeah. Apparently the fight grew to epic proportions and when she stormed out of his place she swore she was going to make him pay. She said he'd see that without her, he had no life at all. It was right at the start of finals week and he said he decided he just had to buckle down and get through his exams and then try to talk to her after she cooled off some."

"Which he never got a chance to," Mark said.

"Nope. One day he was studying with his roommate and he just couldn't keep his eyes open. He thought he'd been going at it too hard, not getting enough sleep. He decided to lay down on the couch for an hour before dinner. As he was drifting off to sleep he heard Lizzie's voice saying an incantation and he felt all his muscles locking up. He tried to pull himself out of it, but it was like something was physically grabbing him and pulling him down into sleep. He said he could see darkness swallowing him up and the last thing he heard was her laughter."

"Creepy," Jeremiah said.

His phone rang and Mark noticed that they all jumped slightly. He snatched it up. "Hello?"

"It's Liam. We've been all over the place, taken fingerprints. Not sure if we'll be able to pick up anything that way, what with all the volunteers who are touching these cages and things every week."

"At least we can try."

"Yes. The scary part is that they didn't even try to hide what they were after. There was no attempt to even make it look like vandalism or some random act," Liam said. "Whoever took those cats didn't care if people knew that was exactly what they were doing."

"How many cats again?"

"Six. Four adults and two kittens. We've got pictures of them all and they've all already been chipped so if they show up, we'll know."

"No owners, though, right?"

"Nope. These were six cats just hoping for a home."

"Well, we'll do what we can to see they still have that chance," Mark said.

"Time to fill me in?"

"Yeah, come over to the hospital and see me. I'm in Room 311."

"I'll be there shortly."

"Sorry, Liam. Did I ruin your weekend plans?"

"Yeah, but it's okay. I had a ticket to go see Doctor Geek's Science Fair, but they're putting those on in different parts of the country, so hopefully I can see it somewhere else soon."

"Good, because vacation is officially over."

"Understood."

Mark hung up. "Six cats. No leads yet." He sighed and looked at Trina. "Samuel really thinks Lizzie cursed him?"

"He absolutely believes it," she confirmed.

"And what do we believe?" he asked.

"Excuse me?" Trina countered, eyes widening slightly.

"Curses? Real? Not?" he let his eyes drift over to Jeremiah. "What about it, Rabbi? Can these things happen?"

Jeremiah shook his head. "I don't know what to tell you. My experience tells me no, but I do try to keep an open mind to the spiritual forces at work around us. It could be possible. It's possible that she didn't curse him, but that part of him believed it so completely that she might as well have."

"Great," Mark grumbled. "Okay, anything else Trina?"

She shook her head.

"Jeremiah, you're up."

"One of the girls at church, Brenda, talked to Cindy and Wildman. Turns out she was good friends with Cheyenne, the first victim, and really torn up about it. She pointed a finger at Cheyenne's older sister, Lacey, saying she was the only one who wouldn't hesitate to hurt Cheyenne. Brenda said she believed Lacey was the killer."

"Interesting," Mark said, narrowing his eyes. "Cheyenne's parents didn't even mention that they had another daughter. I wonder if they were thinking the same thing and were trying to cover for her?"

"Worth doing some digging," Trina suggested.

Mark's phone rang again and he answered it. As he listened to Liam he felt his blood pressure rising. At last he was off the call and he stared grimly at the other two.

"I have to get out of here."

Jeremiah rolled his eyes. "We've already been through that once, remember?"

Mark shook his head. "You don't understand. They found another body."

As Jeremiah drove home that evening he was deeply frustrated. There had been things at the synagogue he'd had to take care of. He'd had to leave the hospital in the middle of Mark trying to persuade the doctor to discharge him. As Jeremiah himself had pointed out, he'd spent the majority of the week at Mark's work sites instead of his own.

Marie had been in a mood which hadn't helped and as he took care of all the things that were piled up on his desk he kept thinking that none of them was as important as stopping the monster that was sacrificing young women. Several times he had to take a deep breath and remind himself that he had chosen to be a Rabbi and not a cop and that sometimes he just had to leave things to the professionals.

Trina was interesting. She was hiding something, that much was easy to see. What it was that she was hiding was much more uncertain. Still, he knew that she wanted to catch the person or persons behind these murders just as much as the rest of them.

Mark had called him in the late afternoon. Apparently he had managed to finally secure his release from the hospital, this time with doctor consent, even if it was given grudgingly. He had described the third crime scene for him. This time an abandoned store had served as the scene. All the details about the layout of the body had been the same. The markings appeared to be the same as well. It had also struck Jeremiah that both the second and third location were not that far from the first. He kept thinking there was something significant about that, something convenient for the killer.

Mark had been heading home after the crime scene and had confessed how much he wasn't looking forward to that. Traci still wouldn't return his calls. Jeremiah felt for him. Jeremiah promised Mark that he'd try and decipher the markings on the bodies later that night and give him a call in the morning.

After feeding Captain and himself he settled down at the computer with the file Mark had given him with the pictures of the symbols on the first girl's body. It took hours but he finally was able to get the rough meanings of each of them thanks to a couple of old books he'd carried with him for years and the help of his computer search engine. He had planned to call Mark in the morning with his findings, but as he looked it all over he realized that this probably shouldn't wait.

"Hello?" the Detective answered the phone, slurring the word. Jeremiah wasn't sure if he'd woken him or if it was still the ill effects of the poison his body was recovering from.

"I know what the symbols mean."

"Yeah, what?" Mark said, sounding like he was struggling to pull himself together.

"There are symbols for life and death from various ancient writing systems, but there are also words written in ancient Sumerian that look like they're appearing throughout the body at regular intervals, almost like an incantation."

"What does it say?"

"Accept offering one of eight in exchange life eternal."

"What?" Mark asked, now sounding thoroughly awake.

"You heard me. I want to see a picture of the markings on the second and third girls, but if I'm right, there are five more that are marked for death."

There was silence on the other end.

"Mark, are you there?"

"Yeah. Meet me at the Starbucks across from the police station in fifteen minutes. We need to get ahead of this now."

When Jeremiah made it to the coffee house he discovered Mark and Trina already huddled at a table, both looking ashen.

"Is it true what you found?" Trina asked before Jeremiah could even sit down.

He nodded.

"And you're sure it's Sumerian?"

"Yes. Why?"

"I've heard about a Sumerian spell designed to do what you're saying, give a kind of immortality but at the cost of eight other lives. I've seen references to it in some obscure old manuscripts, but I've never seen an actual copy of the spell itself."

"How would someone even go about finding something like that?" Mark asked, voice full of misery.

"Simple. They either spent a tremendous amount of time looking for it or they stumbled across it by complete accident," Trina answered.

"What do you know of the spell?" Jeremiah asked.

"Hold it, just one minute. Are we actually saying we believe in magic and spells and all this hoodoo?" Mark asked. "Because, when I asked earlier no one wanted to say so."

"Whether or not it's real is immaterial," Trina said. "Someone out there believes it is and they're not going to stop killing innocent people until they think they've accomplished what they set out to do."

"Valid point," Mark said.

"So, back to my question," Jeremiah said.

"I know only this, that it takes eight people to make the sacrifice and that those eight people have to be connected in some way to the people performing the ritual."

"What do you mean connected?" Mark asked.

"The sacrifices have to be personal, they can't be just random people. It was probably an attempt to make sure that there was a great personal cost to this spell so that only those who were most committed would actually follow through."

"So, Michelle was killed because she was Lizzie's roommate?"

198

Trina nodded. "It is possible."

"So we need to find out who might be the dark witch that's connected to Cheyenne and then maybe we can follow their trail to Lizzie," Mark said.

"What if it is her sister Lacey? What if she's the dark witch?" Jeremiah asked.

"We have to find Lacey," Trina said.

"Way ahead of you," Mark answered as he whipped out his notepad. He'd had his hands too busy to follow up on the Lacey lead earlier and now he was regretting it. A minute later the phone over at Cheyenne's parents' house was ringing. The mom answered, clearly having been awoken.

"I'm sorry, ma'am, this is Detective Walters. I apologize for calling so late. It's very important that I speak with your daughter Lacey, though."

"Then I suggest you call her," the woman said, sounding upset.

"If you would be so kind to give me her phone number and address I'd be happy to contact her directly."

"Just a minute."

Five minutes later she finally came back on the line and he copied down the information she gave him. He hung up and grabbed his coffee. "She lives in an apartment complex just off campus. Let's get over there and see if we can't stop ourselves a witch."

They all piled in Mark's car and he used the lights and siren to blast his way across town. He turned them both off when he got a few blocks away from the apartment building.

"No need to let her know we're coming," Mark said.

Minutes later he was parking in front of her building. "She's apartment 312. Should be on the third floor," Mark commented as he headed for the stairs. He was moving slow. He had to admit that he still wasn't operating at full capacity. He refused to go as far as admitting that the doctor would have been right to force him to stay in the hospital another day or two. He didn't have time for that. He had a killer to stop and a wife to get back.

As Mark passed beneath one of the street lights a blond haired girl walked by him, wearing a gray university sweatshirt. She gazed at him with abnormally large eyes that matched the color of the T-shirt. She smiled at him and kept walking.

He, Trina, and Jeremiah made it to the stairs. Trina started up, followed by Jeremiah. Something was bothering Mark, though, and he couldn't quite put his finger on it. He stayed at the bottom for a moment, hesitating with his foot on the stair. It was more than just the fact that he was tired and didn't want to climb.

"What is it?" Jeremiah asked, turning around.

That's when it hit him. "Freaky Eyes," he blurted out.

"What?"

"That was the girl Lizzie told her roommate about."

He turned and sprinted back toward the parking lot, eyes darting back and forth as he looked for the girl in the sweatshirt. Jeremiah passed him easily and Mark came to a halt as he watched the rabbi run partway down the street in one direction then turn and run back. He shook his head and Mark cursed. She was gone and he had no idea which direction to even look for her. Furious at himself he headed back to the apartment building, Jeremiah a couple steps ahead of him.

When Mark finally made it up the three flights of stairs he was dizzy and out of breath. He probably should have stayed in the hospital and trusted Liam to be his eyes and ears. That was part of his problem, though. He always preferred to do things himself when he could. That drive had led him back to that basement and caused Traci to leave him.

He tried to push those thoughts from his mind. They weren't helpful at the moment and he needed to focus.

Trina and Jeremiah were already inside apartment 312, although he did not ask how. Trina was holding up a cloak and what looked like a ceremonial dagger. Jeremiah on the other hand appeared to be transfixed by something on the television.

"This is her place," Trina said.

Mark swore. "We missed her. She was the girl in the sweatshirt who walked right past us. How are we supposed to find her now?"

"That's not our only problem," Jeremiah said quietly.

"What are you talking about?"

"You should come look at this."

Mark and Trina walked over to join Jeremiah in front of the television.

"You remember how you said a while back that we need to get ahead of this?"

"Yes."

"We're too late," Jeremiah said.

It was a clip from the late news and Mark recognized the dilapidated house behind the newscaster. He didn't have to read the scroll at the bottom to realize it was bad, but he read it anyway.

Witch coven performing human sacrifices in Pine Springs, CA. Police have no leads.

"How did this get out?" Jeremiah asked.

"No clue," Mark admitted as the horror of it all flooded through him. "None of my people would have talked."

"Well, someone has. And now we're all in for it."

19

National media descended the next morning and it threw them all into chaos as predicted. Cindy was just grateful that both she and Jeremiah seemed to be miraculously escaping attention. Mark and Trina, on the other hand, were right in the middle of it.

Jeremiah expressed concern that sooner or later the synagogue could get sucked in if the reporters discovered that one of the kids from there had run away a few days earlier. More than that, though, he was starting to express concern that Meghan might not have actually run away, but that she had been snatched.

Cindy wasn't sure which was worse, the thought that Meghan's life might be in danger or that someone close to the girl was a dark witch who was willing to sacrifice her.

When Sunday rolled around she was grateful to find that no reporters had descended on the church. She was also more than a little surprised to find out how many of the kids had come with their work clothes, still prepared to spend the day finishing the haunted house. She and Jeremiah lent their efforts as well and as she watched the kids she quickly realized that many of them were scared about what was happening in Pine Springs but that they were focusing on the haunted house to keep their minds off of the real world horrors.

"Rabbi," one of the kids said, coming up to them while they were sitting down taking a break and drinking sodas.

"What is it, Zac?"

"You are coming to our dress rehearsal Tuesday night, right? A lot of us are counting on you to give us some last minute pointers. We've got some parents coming through as guests and we want to make sure we scare them silly."

"I wouldn't miss it, Zac," Jeremiah said with a smile.

Zac nodded solemnly and turned back to the others. "Told you he's coming!" he bellowed, before running off.

"That was subtle," Cindy said, barely controlling a laugh.

"He was one of the ones who was with me at Green Pastures," Jeremiah said. "Apparently I made an impression."

"You know that's one of the things we haven't talked about in light of everything I now know about you," she said thoughtfully.

"We can, if you want. These kids don't seem like they're going to be forgetting any time soon."

"It's a bit memorable when someone saves your life. At least, that's what I've heard," she said, teasing a little.

He grinned at her and one of the younger boys who was resting nearby stared at them and then made a kissy face.

"Get back to work!" Jeremiah barked at him.

The kid jumped up and ran over to help two other boys with a black curtain they were trying to hang.

"You're coming to the dress rehearsal, right?" Jeremiah asked her.

"Oh no, count me out. Haunted houses are definitely not my thing."

"But the kids have worked so hard on it."

"Tell you what, I'll take a look at some of the scenes today when they've got it all up and while all the lights are still on and no one is going to jump out at me."

"Fair enough."

"You sound pretty proud of them and what they're doing. I thought you didn't want to be involved," she said.

Jeremiah sighed. "It's...complicated."

Wildman was in his glory, running here, there, and everywhere. One minute he was shouting directions, the next he was giving encouragement. He was quoting the scriptures from which some of their scenes had been taken with fiendish glee the rest of the time. She hoped for his sake that everything went well. Halloween itself was on Saturday night and the kids were going to be running the attraction Thursday, Friday, and Saturday.

Thinking about Halloween made her think of her costume which led her to wondering what Jeremiah had decided to go as. She was just about to ask him when a girl walked up to him, clearly distressed.

"What's wrong, Sarah?" he asked.

She recognized the name. This was the girl whose younger sister was missing.

"Brenda was supposed to be here today and she hasn't shown up."

"Brenda's been through a lot this week, maybe she was exhausted and slept in," Cindy said gently.

Sarah shook her head. "I talked to her this morning while she was getting ready for church. I've been calling her all afternoon and she's not picking up. This haunted house has been the only thing keeping her going. Me, too," she admitted quietly.

Cindy impulsively stood up and hugged the girl. "Tell you what? After we're all done here Pastor Wyman and I will go check on her, okay?"

"Thank you," Sarah said.

True to her word, Cindy did walk through the maze immediately after the last kids had been picked up. Even with the lights on and no one jumping out at her it was scary. When she emerged out the other end she gave Wildman the thumbs up.

"Now imagine it dark with fog and people," he said enthusiastically.

"No, I'm good imagining it just as it is now," she said.

They locked up the church campus and then headed out to the parking lot with Jeremiah. Daves's car was out of the shop so he offered to drive and then drop Cindy back off at the church. She couldn't be sure, but it almost looked like Jeremiah was glaring at Mark again. She decided she had to be crazy.

"Checking in on Brenda is a nice thing," Dave said once they were on the road.

"I hope so. I know she didn't want us dropping her off at home the other day because her family doesn't understand her participation at church. Still, Sarah's worried and that made me worried."

"Given that she just lost a friend less than a week ago I think we're doing the right thing. Hopefully her family will see that as well. Who knows, maybe they actually decided to do something nice for her today. A family outing or something."

"Could be," Cindy said, although she kind of doubted it.

After a few minutes they turned onto Brenda's street. Cindy stared out the window at the rundown homes, remembering her first trip here with Brenda, two other girls, and the Thanksgiving dinner. She remembered how rundown it had been. Somehow, though, things were looking far too familiar, as if it hadn't been nearly two years since she'd seen some of the houses she was driving by.

As Dave pulled over to the curb she looked farther down the street and suddenly it hit her. They were on the same street as the house where Cheyenne had been killed.

The hair stood up all over her body at the realization and she gasped.

"What's wrong?" Dave asked.

She pointed up the street. "The house where Cheyenne was found dead is just a block that way."

"Oh man, are you sure?" Dave asked, alarm filling his voice.

"Yes."

"I hope she doesn't know that, know how close her friend was when she died," he said.

Cindy, on the other hand, hoped just the opposite. She hoped Brenda knew how close she was to danger.

Dave got out of the car and Cindy followed slowly, wishing she'd never promised Sarah that she would come here. She licked her dry lips and forced herself to turn and look at Brenda's house.

It was as though she could still sense the other house, just a short distance away, darkness reaching out from it like tendrils seeking to ensnare any who got too close.

Your imagination is running away with you! she scolded herself.

They made it to the door and Dave knocked. It opened a minute later and an older woman Cindy vaguely recognized was standing there, drying her hands on a faded apron. "Can I help you?"

"Yes, a friend of Brenda's just wanted us to check in and make sure she was okay. We know that she's suffered a loss this week and we wanted to see how she was doing," Dave said, clearly trying to just come out and avoid saying that they worked at the church.

"Heck if I know. You could ask her yourself if she was here."

"She's not?" Cindy asked.

"Nah. She hasn't been here since early this morning. She headed to the bus stop down on the corner. She goes to some church on Sundays. Don't know why. Guess she got it in her head that somehow God's real or something."

"What time do you expect her back?" Dave asked.

The woman shrugged. "Whenever she gets here, I guess."

There was a crash in the other room. "Excuse me, I've got other kids to worry about at the moment," she said. "Boys!" she shouted as she closed the door.

"I don't like this," Cindy admitted as she and Dave walked back to the sidewalk.

"Me either. Let's take a look at the bus stop."

A feeling of dread settled in the pit of Cindy's stomach as she realized the bus stop was even closer to the creepy house than Brenda's home was. She could feel her heart beginning to pound as they walked toward it.

Once there they looked around, but Cindy didn't even know what they were looking for. Her eyes began to water and a moment later she sneezed.

"Bless you," Dave said.

"Sarah told us that Brenda hadn't been answering her phone since this morning," Cindy said.

"I have her number," Dave said, pulling out his phone. He pushed a couple of buttons and a moment later there was a shrill ringing sound from just a couple of feet away. Seconds later Cindy found a phone, face down in a bit of scraggly grass and half pressed into the dirt.

She sneezed harder as she picked it up.

"Why is her phone here?" Dave asked, voice filling with alarm.

Cindy sneezed again, so hard this time that she almost dropped the phone and her eyes began to water more. "What is that smell?" she asked.

"I don't know."

With a sudden sinking sensation she realized she did. It was the same thing she had smelled in the basement of the creepy house. Burnt acacia. She backpedaled away from the area, still holding Brenda's phone with three fingers. She shouldn't have even picked it up, she realized belatedly.

"Dave, call 911," she said.

"Why?"

"Because Brenda's been kidnapped by the same people who killed Cheyenne."

20

Mark was living in his own personal hell. Even during the Passion Week killings, they'd somehow managed to avoid national press attention. Now he had reporters dogging his steps, questioning his every move. It was making it hard to do his job. Trina was in the same boat. When they'd gotten the call about Brenda being kidnapped, Mark knew things were just going to get worse.

It was Sunday night and they were at an all-night restaurant, each of them getting their first real meal of the day and trying to figure out what they could from the few facts they had.

"So, eight coven members and eight sacrifices, one person that's connected to each coven member," Mark said.

"Yes," Trina said.

"We know Lacey's sacrifice was Cheyenne. Lizzie's sacrifice was Michelle."

"You know there is still a chance that she might not be a willing participant," Trina said.

"I hope to heaven you're right, but, at least we can cross them off the list."

He actually was making a list. It was like some old time logic puzzle where you had to connect up the people in the left column with the people in the right column through a series of clues.

He looked at the rest of the names in the left column, the victims or intended ones. "So, that leaves the new girl..." he drifted off in horror realizing he was so exhausted he couldn't even remember the name of victim number three.

"Brit."

"That's right, Brit. We've also got Brenda and potentially Meghan."

"I'd say probably."

"Which leaves three people who we don't know of who are either dead or missing or about to become dead or missing.'

"Yes."

"And we know the names of two of the coven members, and descriptions for two more: Trust Fund Brat and Creepy Tall Guy. That leaves four unknown coven members."

"So, the question is, can we match up whoever Trust Fund Brat and Creepy Tall Guy are with Brit, Brenda, or Meghan?"

"That is the question, isn't it?" Mark said. "Liam spent all day interviewing families while I was tied up with the press. Brit, Brenda, and Meghan all lived at home, so no roommates to worry about."

"It could be friends from school," Trina said. She took a deep breath. "Or even from the church or the synagogue."

"I do not even want to go there," Mark said, feeling sick inside at the very thought.

"Okay, let's stick with families for the moment. Let's break it down."

"Brenda's family is dirt poor, painfully so. I don't see there being any connection to a Trust Fund Brat there, at least not anyone who would be close enough to make the sacrifice count."

"Okay, what about Brit?" Trina asked.

"Her family was pretty poor as well."

"Then let's take a look at Meghan."

Mark nodded. "Meghan's family is well-off, not what you'd call wildly wealthy, but not hurting."

"And extended family?"

Mark paused. "You know, I'm not sure, but I know someone who might."

He got out his phone and called Jeremiah, way beyond caring that at one in the morning he'd probably be waking him up.

"What's happened?" Jeremiah said as he answered the phone.

"Question. Meghan's family, any rich cousins or anything?"

"I don't think they have any cousins in the synagogue, so I wouldn't know."

"Think, please."

"Okay. Wait."

"Yes?" Mark asked hopefully.

"At the prayer vigil for her at the synagogue I did notice a very expensive car in the parking lot. I was introduced to an older woman, an aunt, who was wearing designer clothes. So was her daughter who spent the entire time looking irritated which I thought was pretty rude."

"Trust fund brat!" Mark said triumphantly.

"What?"

"One of the coven members, that was her nickname. Do you know the names of these people?"

"Aunt Sylvia, that's all I heard."

"That's good enough. I'll call Meghan's family right now."

Mark hung up the phone and within a minute was talking to Meghan's mom. The woman had clearly still been awake and her voice was sick with worry. She readily provided the contact information for her sister-in-law without even asking questions. She even confirmed that Sylvia's daughter, Casey, did indeed live with her even though she was in college.

After hanging up with her Mark filled Trina in. "We need to get over there and find Casey and try and make her talk. People like that are going to have a lawyer on stand-by, though."

"I can be very persuasive," Trina said, eyes narrowing.

"No doubt. What we really need, though, is a search warrant so we don't lose any evidence. What we've got, though, is so thin even I wouldn't give me a search warrant."

Trina smiled. "I've got that covered."

"How?"

"Like I said, I can be very persuasive. While I'm taking care of that call Liam and tell him to meet us at the house with a bunch of officers and a forensics team."

She pulled out her phone, stood and walked toward the front of the restaurant while Mark brought Liam up to speed. A minute later she was back.

"Tell Liam to meet us at the house in thirty minutes. That will just give us enough time to stop and pick up the search warrant."

Mark relayed the information then hung up. "How on earth did you pull that off?"

She lowered her voice slightly. "As I said, I can be very persuasive."

He believed her.

Thirty minutes later, just as she had predicted, they were outside a sprawling mansion with Liam and a dozen other officers. Mark had rung the doorbell and was now waiting, practically holding his breath.

A woman answered a couple minutes later, wearing an expensive looking robe and managing to look both confused and angry at the same time. "What is going on?" she demanded.

Trina stepped forward with the warrant. "Sylvia, we have a warrant to search this house."

Even as the woman gasped in shock officers began flooding inside.

"Ma'am, is your daughter, Casey, home?" Mark asked.

"What is the meaning of this?"

"Mom?"

Mark looked inside and saw a young woman coming down the stairs. Unlike her mother she was dressed. She made it to the bottom of the stairs.

"Casey?" Mark asked, moving past the mother.

Casey took one look at Mark and Trina and bolted to the left. Trina leaped after her and Mark was left to chase after both of them. Casey made it out a back door and was halfway to the street when suddenly she fell, sprawling in the middle of the lawn.

Trina was next to her in a moment, slapping handcuffs on her. When Mark reached them he noted that a tree root on the ground seemed to be what had tripped Casey when she was running. It seemed so odd to see it in the middle of the well-manicured lawn, especially when the nearest tree was a good fifteen feet away. He wasn't about to look a gift horse in the mouth, though. He began reading Casey her rights as Trina hauled the girl to her feet.

They started walking her toward Mark's car. As soon as Mark had finished the spiel, he looked at Casey and growled, "We know you're part of the dark coven sacrificing girls."

"What if I am?" she asked, brazen, mocking.

He was stunned that the first words out of her mouth hadn't been that she wanted her lawyer.

"You needed a personal sacrifice of your own and poor confused, angst ridden Meghan must have been the perfect choice," Trina said.

Casey actually laughed. "Sure, I was the one who grabbed my cousin. Stupid little girl just wanted to get away from home. I provided that. I also got Brenda. I'd met her at that stupid prayer vigil and knew she was friends with Sarah. She recognized me when I offered her a ride to the church and she got right in my car. I knocked her out, tossed her phone, and it was simple."

"You had no connection to her," Mark said. "Which means someone else in your coven must."

They had reached Mark's car. For a moment Casey looked slightly confused. "I want my la-"

She was about to say she wanted her lawyer and then it was all over. They'd have to stop questioning her. Before she could get the entire word out, though, Trina slammed her hand down on the car, startling him and Casey.

"Tell us where the girls are!"

"I don't know!" Casey said, suddenly looking frightened.

Mark believed her and he hated that he did.

"I had Meghan here with me for a couple of days, letting her think she was hiding out. Then when she started talking about going home I had to knock her out. Lacey came and took her somewhere."

"Where?" Trina demanded.

"I swear I don't know!"

"Where would Lacey go if not her apartment?"

"I don't know! I didn't even know she lived in an apartment, I swear. She didn't talk much about herself."

"But you've got her phone number," Mark said.

Casey shook her head. "She had to ditch her phone a couple of days ago. Lizzie had gotten to it. She's called me three times since then, but all from different numbers. I don't have a way to call her back."

"Who are the other members of your coven?" Trina demanded.

"I don't know, Mother recruited them all."

"Wait, your mother?" Mark asked, half-turning toward the house.

"No, our high priestess. That's what she insisted on us calling her. Lacey, Lizzie, another guy and I had broken off from our wiccan group, formed our own coven. We wanted something the other group could never give us."

"Power," Mark said.

Casey nodded. "And we were getting it, but slowly. Then Mother showed up one day several months back. She was from the Santa Cruz area. Something had happened to her coven up there though she never talked about it."

Trina actually jerked and Mark wondered if she knew something about that. He'd have to ask her later.

"Mother said that we could get power, real power. And she was right. The things I've seen! Then she told us about this amazing spell."

"Immortality," Trina said.

"Yes. But she said that it would take sacrifice and that we'd need three more coven members. She recruited them personally. The last one joined us a few weeks ago. Then, we were ready."

"What are their names?" Mark demanded.

"I don't know! We all tried to avoid names and the more intense it got the better an idea that seemed."

"So, describe them to us," Trina said.

"There were two guys, one older and one younger. The younger one's my age and the older one has gray hair but he's weird, you know. It's like some days he looks fifty and some days he looks thirty. I don't know how old he really is. She also brought in another girl, she's like nineteen or twenty. We called her Smoking Girl."

"Why?"

"Because she's a chain smoker."

"Who is Creepy Tall Guy?" Trina asked.

"I don't know his real name! He was with us in the wiccan coven for just a couple of weeks and came with us when Lacey, Lizzie, and I broke away."

"Which one did you kidnap Brenda for?" Mark asked.

Casey opened her mouth then shut it. Her entire body shuddered. "I want my la-"

"Answer the question!" Trina screamed in her face.

Casey blinked, and then nodded slowly. "I kidnapped her for Smoking Girl."

"How are she and Brenda related?" Mark asked.

"I don't know. I just know that Brenda was needed for her."

"Brit, who was she for?" Mark asked.

"One of the two new guys."

"There are three others. Mother's sacrifice, Creepy Tall Guy's sacrifice, and the other new guy's sacrifice. Have those people been kidnapped yet?"

Casey smirked. "Mother's sacrifice is already dead. He was the first, and you guys still haven't found him."

Mark felt like he'd been punched in the gut. "What?"

Casey nodded. "Killed him a week before Cheyenne."

"Where?"

"Don't know. Mother drove. We were all crammed into a van and we couldn't see out. When we got there, he was already there, chained up. We just had to perform the ritual. That was when she freaked out."

"Who?" Trina asked.

"Lizzie. Apparently she thought the whole "death thing" was supposed to be symbolic. Boy was she stupid. Once she realized what was going on she tried to back out. But no one leaves the coven. Funny thing about the ritual. You just need eight coven members to make it happen, not all of them have to be conscious for it."

Mark felt himself sag in relief, but he refused to show it outwardly. "So, that's when the group kidnapped Lizzie."

Casey nodded. "Left her there, tied up in the same room as the body. Mother's been checking on her."

"Is that where they're keeping the other sacrifices?"

Casey shrugged. "Don't know."

"And what about the other two? Have they been taken yet?"

"Don't know."

Something seemed to be happening. Casey's eyes were getting glassy and it was like she was shutting down.

"Where's the next sacrifice supposed to take place?" he asked.

"Don't know."

"When?"

"Don't know."

"Who?"

"Don't know."

He looked into her eyes and it was as though she had somehow checked out.

"She's done. She's told us everything she knows," Trina said, her voice hoarse sounding.

Mark opened the back door of his car and Trina literally gave Casey a tiny push. The girl's body crumpled, falling forward into the backseat.

"Fried," Trina muttered under her breath, sounding disgusted.

"You think she was on something?" Mark asked.

"What?" Trina looked up at him, almost looking surprised to see him standing there like he had somehow startled her when she was in deep thought.

"You think she was on drugs or something?" he reiterated.

"No. I just think...never mind, I'm just talking to myself."

"It's been a long day for both of us," he said.

The sound of squealing tires caused Mark to jerk his head up and look down the street. A news van was shooting around the corner and came careening down the street.

"It's about to get a lot longer," he muttered.

"Let's get out of here while we can. We'll apologize to Liam later," Trina said, quickly getting into the front seat.

"Yeah, I think you're right," Mark said.

Casey's behavior at the end was creeping him out. The sooner they got her down to the precinct and booked the better he'd feel. Then they could focus on who connected with Brenda could be Smoking Girl. He yawned and realized he was actually nodding off. Some sleep somewhere in there might be a good thing, too.

It was Monday morning and Cindy sat in her car in the parking lot, dreading going into work even more than she usually did on a Monday. It was going to be a week of raving lunatics, homicidal maniacs, and bloodthirsty monsters. And that was just counting the people at church. After a minute of quietly contemplating the drawbacks of quitting and being unemployed she forced herself out of the car.

At least there were no reporters at the church. It seemed like the one place there weren't reporters these days. It was the one silver lining in the whole mess. She had stayed up half the night praying for Brenda, Meghan, and anyone else who might be in danger and she was beyond tired.

She trudged toward the gate, forcing one weary foot in front of the other. She had to get some rest soon. This was getting ridiculous. She unlocked the gate as she contemplated what horrors awaited her in the office. She wasn't ready to deal with them, especially not until she'd had some caffeine. She'd forgotten to pick up soda at the store the night before and she was running on empty in that area.

She made her way over to the sanctuary. There was going to be an early morning prayer meeting in there and she wanted to make sure everything looked presentable. She unlocked the door and made her way toward the light switch. Before she reached it her foot caught on something and she staggered sideways, crashing into the wall. She managed to keep her feet.

Cindy reached out with a shaking hand and found the switch. A moment later the lights came on and she looked down. The body of a man was sprawled face down on the ground, a hangman's noose knotted around his neck.

21

Cindy choked back the scream that was rising in her throat even as her mind was frantically repeating the words *Not again!* over and over. She was having flashbacks to the first time she'd tripped over a body on the sanctuary floor. There was something different this time even though she was struggling to put her finger on what it was.

She was about to reach down and tug on the man's trousers when it hit her. Something seemed off about his proportions. A terrible suspicion dawned on her and she grabbed one of the legs which lifted off the ground with ease.

With a disgusted grunt she flipped the entire body over. It was fake, a Halloween prop that the kids must have been prepping for their haunted house. The face was distorted with bulging eyes and tongue. It was grotesque but seen from this angle not at all realistic looking.

She closed her eyes for a moment struggling to calm her nerves. She had thought for sure that she was going to be calling Mark because she had managed to trip over another dead body. She was fairly certain she would never have lived that one down. She was immensely grateful that wasn't the case, though. The church had already seen its fair share of death and didn't need any more. Then again, neither did she.

She was going to have to tell Dave that his kids needed to be more careful with their props, though. Someone could have been injured or badly frightened. They were all very lucky that she had been the one who had tripped over it. Even that she realized was ironic. So much had changed in her life since that first body in the sanctuary. Looking back she marveled at it all even as she picked up the mannequin and carried him to the office.

Once inside she briefly considered hanging him from one of the light fixtures before realizing that wasn't a good idea. The fact that she had even contemplated it though was proof of just how different life was than it had been a couple of years ago. It was also proof that she'd had too little sleep and her judgment was seriously impaired. She really did need some caffeine as fast as possible.

Mark had only managed to get a couple of hours sleep. By the time he'd made it home the sun had been coming up. He blamed the fact that he had been half-awake on that, but in his heart he knew it was because he couldn't sleep in the bed without Traci. The worst part was that she still wasn't returning his phone calls.

He knew that she and the kids and Buster were at Amber's house so at least he knew they were safe. He had thought about going there but had images of the press somehow following him and just making things worse.

Trina had done a great job procuring the search warrant the night before. Maybe she could convince a judge to issue an injunction against the reporters who were hounding them. It was a dream at any rate.

He knew they weren't going to get any more information out of Casey. After they'd gotten her booked he'd had to call in a psychologist to take a look at her. She seemed to have just checked out, like she was barely there, and only capable of answering the most rudimentary questions with either "yes" or "don't know". Maybe the stress of it all had gotten to her. He didn't know what was going on inside her head, but to do what she'd done it already had to be full of messed up wiring.

They had found Meghan's phone and some of her other belongings in the house, proof that she was telling the truth about that part. They'd also found some hair and blood in the front seat of her car that should belong to Brenda. Now they just needed to find where they were being held before something happened to them.

His phone rang and his heart skipped a beat when he saw it was Traci calling. He picked up. "Hello?"

"You said in your message this morning that you found out something about Lizzie?"

When he'd gotten home he had left her a message to that effect. He was going to tell her what he knew, but realized that if he didn't then she might actually call him to find out the information. It had worked.

"I did. I found out that she is being held by the coven, and that she was a part of it. The good news, if you can call it that, is that she has not been a party to the murders. When she objected is when they kidnapped her."

"Thank heavens," Traci said. "Wait, I know that sounds weird, she's still in danger and all..."

"I'm just as relieved as you are that Lizzie isn't an accessory to murder," Mark said gently. "I'm still terrified for her, but I'm relieved, too. The girl I used to know would never have been able to hurt someone like that."

"I know. I've just been having the most terrible imagery in my head."

"Me, too. The other thing I discovered is that they can't...get rid of her until they've completed all eight rituals. So, they have four more they have to get through before they could do anything to her. Given that we just captured one of their number, they might not even be able to accomplish those."

"You caught someone?"

"Yes, in the middle of the night. The cousin of the girl everyone thought was a runaway. Unfortunately, she couldn't tell us where Lizzie or the others are being held." He paused. "It's been a rough couple of days and there's a lot more to get through. How are you doing?"

"I don't want to talk about it," she said abruptly.

"Okay, when you do, I want to listen."

"Thanks for letting me know about Lizzie. Bye."

Before he could say anything else she hung up.

Frustrated he sat down on the couch and forced himself to breathe deep. At least she'd called back. He'd gotten to hear her voice. Slowly he straightened as he replayed the conversation in his head. He'd said something important. Casey had told him they could hold the ritual with an unconscious coven member, but that they needed all eight. Unless they were stupid enough to try and break her out of jail that meant things were on hold until they could find someone to take her place.

Mother would be recruiting again and she'd be in a hurry. Just maybe there was someone who could help him figure out some likely candidates.

Half an hour later he was sitting in a coffee shop with Sweater Girl. She was drinking what had to be the most froufrou concoction he'd ever heard of, but he was just grateful she'd agreed to meet. He'd asked her if there was anyone she knew in her coven or in the larger wicca community that she could think of who might be tempted by the dark side.

She was sitting, thinking as she sipped her drink, and he was trying to be patient.

While he was waiting he was thinking. He assumed that a new sacrifice would have to be chosen who had a connection to whoever the new coven member was. That didn't just mean that they'd let Meghan go, though. He guessed that they'd keep her and Lizzie alive until they had completed the eighth sacrifice and then kill them, too. Of course, if they believed their ritual was real and Lizzie as well as them would suddenly become immortal because of it, he wasn't sure how they planned on getting rid of her. He'd learned a long time ago, though, not to question the logic of madmen.

Finally she put her cup down. "This is going to sound crazy."

"I love crazy as long as it gets me somewhere," Mark said.

"I really hate to say this, but the person that keeps popping into my mind is Samuel."

"The guy who just got out of the coma?" Mark said in surprise.

"Yeah, I know, it sounds crazy. It's just...I've talked to him a couple of times in the past few days and he's angry. I mean, really angry. He was angry that he'd lost two years of his life and he was looking to find a way to get that time back and to punish Lizzie."

"So, not so much into the doing no harm to others anymore?"

"Exactly. I mean, he's really messed up. I've tried to talk with him, get him some help, but he just keeps getting worse. I think it's hard because he doesn't actually have any family to help him through it either."

"So, he might be open to a proposition from a dark witch?"

"I hate to say it, but he's the only one I know who would be. I mean, I'm sure there are other angry, hurting people in this town, but that's the one my money would be on."

"He should be in the hospital," Mark mused. "All that muscle atrophy and everything he'll need physical therapy for quite a while."

"Plus, no family to push for him to come home," she added.

He nodded and stood. "Thank you very much for your help."

"Thank you for finding my neighbor's cat. I just hope you find mine."

"I'll do my best," he said, wincing inwardly.

From the coffee shop he headed straight for the hospital. It was likely that Mother would know something about Samuel since the coma he was in was supposedly caused by Lizzie and the others could easily have bragged about that at some point.

When he walked into the ward where Samuel had been his bed was empty. He stopped and then realized that this was where the coma patients were and they would probably have moved him somewhere else in the hospital. As he headed out of the room he hailed a nurse who was walking by.

"Hi, I'm Detective Walters and I'm looking for Samuel Bannerman."

"Oh, you just missed him. He checked out of the hospital a couple of hours ago."

"Checked out?" Mark asked, surprised. "Who checked him out?"

The nurse smiled. "It was his Mother."

As the afternoon arrived the excitement and tension at the church became palpable. Kids started showing up as soon as school was out, buzzing about the night's dress rehearsal. When they started getting into costume and makeup the energy went sky high until even Cindy found herself getting jittery with anticipation.

Once it hit five o'clock Jeremiah showed up and the kids got even more amped. Dave was running around like a madman and Cindy realized it was a good thing she had agreed to stay and help.

Finished with one errand she headed to the back door of the gym which was closest. There just outside she ran into Zac and Sarah. Sarah was on the ground, her long hair stretched out straight above her head. Around her were a number of cans of white Halloween hair coloring spray and also an industrial can of regular hairspray, extra hold. Zac had a brush in one hand and was plugging a hair dryer into a socket with the other.

"What are you two doing?" Cindy asked, at a loss.

"Zac's giving me hair that stands straight up, like the Bride of Frankenstein although obviously I'm not her."

"Obviously," Cindy said.

She walked into the gym shaking her head and found Wildman waving his arms around and directing people. He had a massive thermos in his left hand. He brought it to his lips and then lowered it with a look of disgust on his face.

"What's wrong?" Cindy asked.

"Out of water," he mumbled.

She took the thermos from him. "That's easily enough fixed. What else do you need? Did you even eat anything today?"

"Yeah, I had something at lunch," he said distractedly.

"Okay, good. I'll be back with some water."

She exited the front of the gym and made her way to the water fountains. To her disgust it turned out the water pressure was too low in them for some reason. She'd have to say something in the morning and get those fixed. There was another set clear on the other side of the church which she trudged toward.

Once she had filled the thermos she headed back. She walked into the gym and looked for Wildman who wasn't where she'd last seen him. She walked further into the room and a sudden stench assaulted her. She looked around quickly. It smelled like something was burning. She took a few steps toward the back of the gym and it seemed to grow stronger. Then she heard a muffled exclamation coming from outside.

She ran to the back door. She looked out and saw that Zac was standing with a stricken look on his face. There on the ground was Sarah and her hair was on fire.

22

With a shout Cindy dumped the thermos of water on top of the burning hair and then stamped out the embers.

"I don't know what happened!" Zac burst out.

"My guess? You got the really hot part of the blow dryer too close to some hair that was loaded down with hairspray," Cindy said, panting.

"You burned my hair?" Sarah asked, sitting up with a stricken look on her face.

"I don't think he got it too bad," Cindy said, forcing a smile. "Besides, now you can be the awesome girl whose hair was on fire. Maybe you'll become your own urban legend."

The girl stared at her wide-eyed for a moment then burst into a grin. "Cool!"

Cindy let out a sigh of relief. That could have so easily gone the other way. "Here, let me help you get it sorted out." She handed the thermos to Zac. "Fill this with water, find Wildman and give this to him, please."

Zac nodded and disappeared inside. She didn't blame him. If she'd been the one to set Sarah's hair on fire she'd be running.

When Jeremiah made it next door to the church he had discovered a level of chaos that he hadn't seen in a long time. It was like a war zone. Wildman looked like he was going to have some sort of attack and collapse. After taking it all in Jeremiah realized that the best way he could help was by taking charge of the inside of the maze.

He had announced that once people were done with hair and makeup they were to report inside the maze to him. He dropped the lighting level in there, but they wouldn't turn on the fog machines until just before they were ready to begin. With the lowered lighting, though, he could see what their costumes and makeup would look like from a guest's perspective. Then he could put them in their position, make sure they had everything they needed, and give them some last minute scare tips based on their actual location and the things in that environment.

He didn't know how things were outside the maze, but he had them now running smoothly inside with about half the kids in place. As he saw it all coming together he had to admit that Wildman's vision for the haunted house had been amazing. It was like seeing the history of his people come to life in the most terrifying way possible. He had even decided that next year he'd work to see that the synagogue officially partnered with the church on this project.

There would be some people that wouldn't be happy about that, but maybe he could sell it as the synagogue sponsoring the Jewish history portion, also known as the Old Testament as far as the church people went. It was a thought. He shook his head at himself. Look at him planning for next Halloween. It was like he was actually putting down roots.

Mark was sitting in the precinct staring at Daniels. "What do you mean you lost them?"

They had been able to go through footage from hospital security cameras and see a nurse helping Samuel into a car. They even got a pretty good look at the older lady who was driving and they had been able to run the license plates. The car was registered to a Janine Norton from Santa Cruz. They had a name and a face for Mother.

But absolutely no idea where she was still.

Daniels had been able to use his exceptional skills to track the car through half of Pine Springs only to lose it on the outskirts of town. From there it could have gone anywhere. At least he was able to flag the car so that police as far away as Los Angeles would be looking for it.

They had a lot more to go on than they'd had a couple hours earlier, but no matter how many times he reminded himself of that it still felt like they were back at square one.

Cindy walked Sarah into the office after unlocking it. She directed her to the bathroom that usually only staff used so she could have a little privacy and space to try and assess the hair damage. As she was walking over to her desk to grab a pair of scissors to snip off some of the singed edges the phone rang. Without thinking she picked it up.

"Hello?"

A burst of static came through.

"Hello, anyone there?" she asked again.

There was just more static. Sounded like someone was on a cell with terrible reception.

"If you can hear me, you're not coming through at all. You might try hanging up and calling back. The office is actually closed right now, though, so it might be better if you wait until the morning."

There was another burst of static and one word finally came through, "Morning". Then more static and then nothing.

"Okay, I guess they'll be calling back in the morning."

She should have let the machine get it in the first place. She grabbed the scissors and headed to the bathroom. Fortunately, she didn't have to snip too much off.

"I think it's going to be okay," Sarah said with a brave smile.

Cindy squeezed her shoulders. "Absolutely. You'll be the belle of the haunted house."

They left the office and headed back to the gym. It was getting close to time she realized and parents were starting to arrive and mill about outside. Some looked excited, others squeamish. Good for them, though, for coming out to support their kids anyway.

They got into the gym and Sarah headed straight into the haunted house. The line for it was going to start outside the gym and they actually had the exit at the side door that led directly to the parking lot.

That way if you're scared to death you can get out of here fast, Cindy thought to herself.

Dave walked up to her. "I think we're just about ready," he said, taking a deep breath. "I just turned on the fog machines and the scary sound effects. I've got kids organizing the flow into the house. They know to put space between groups for optimal scare. I think I'll be outside for a few getting the parents in line."

"You should interview them afterwards, too."

"Good idea. I've got two other floater kids I can use for that," he said, lighting up. "Jeremiah has volunteered to stay in the maze tonight observing how everything goes so he can make adjustments before we officially open Thursday night."

Cindy nodded. "Sounds like you've got things handled."

"I do."

"What do you need from me?"

"Can you stay with the kids at the front of the haunted house, at least for a bit? Make sure they're leaving ten seconds between groups? Everyone's a bit nervous so an extra pair of eyes around would be great."

"Not a problem." She gave him a swift hug. "Don't worry. It's going to be fantastic."

He nodded and she walked over to stand next to the kids at the entrance to the maze. They looked younger and she figured they were probably Freshmen. They also looked really freaked out which was probably why they were outside of the maze instead of inside.

"Are you ready?" she asked with a smile.

One nodded and the other looked like she might throw up.

"It's going to be great," Cindy said.

Suddenly the gym door opened and a line of parents started walking in. Cindy turned and greeted them all with a smile, although belatedly she realized a scary frown probably would be more appropriate.

They let the first group in and within seconds they could hear screaming. The kids beamed excitedly and the next group of waiting parents looked a little sick. The kids kept right on mark, sending the next group in ten seconds after the first one. By the fourth group they'd definitely hit their rhythm and Cindy was relieved that they didn't actually need her. Although she would tell Dave that it would probably be a good idea to have one adult, ideally a big tough looking guy, stationed at the front in case people got rowdy on the real nights. She smirked. Maybe she'd volunteer Jeremiah for the job the first two. The last night, though, they'd be at the Halloween party.

More and more screams started emanating from the haunted house so she guessed that the kids inside were really getting into the groove as far as knowing when to jump out at people. Jeremiah should be proud from the sounds of things.

They were about halfway through the number of adults she'd seen outside. It looked like it was going to be a successful dress rehearsal and probably over in another few minutes.

The next group went and a lone man stepped up to the line. There was something odd about him. He was old, but yet not in some weird way and she found herself trying to guess his age. There was something else about him that was bothering her, though, and she struggled to put her finger on it.

Acacia. The man smelled like burnt acacia. Cindy locked eyes with him. Something in her face must have given her away because a moment later he bolted into the maze.

"Stop!" she screamed, leaping forward.

And suddenly she was exactly where she didn't want to be, running through the haunted house. All the guy had to do was make it to the end and he was in the parking lot and gone. She shouted for someone to stop him but quickly realized no one was going to hear her over the sound effects and the screams.

She was in the Egyptian plagues scene, trying to focus on the figure ahead of her in the fog. She could see blood rolling down the walls and something wet that she hoped wasn't blood was dripping all over her from above. She twisted around a corner and plague victim leaped out at her.

She screamed, but forced herself to keep running instead of spinning to a halt and beckpedaling like she wanted to.

Jeremiah. He was somewhere in here. He could help her if she could just find him. "Jeremiah!" she screamed at the top of her lungs as she ran.

She rounded another corner and a blast of hot air hit her in the face. Up and down the corridor there were fake flames and people wandering about with what looked like burned and melting flesh falling off their faces. Her heart started pounding even harder but she flew forward screaming, "Send Jeremiah to get me!" She hoped that someone would hear her and get him. Surely the kids would know where he was, but she couldn't stop to ask. She had to keep the man in her sights.

They raced through the maze, passing clusters of laughing or screaming parents. When they reached the Samson scene and the floor was shaking beneath her Cindy stumbled, but managed to keep her feet. It had slowed the man down, too, and she managed to close the gap between them slightly as they rocketed into the middle of demon central complete with the animatronic pig that Dave had described squealing and looking demonic in its own right.

This section was by far the hardest to get through and she kept jumping and flinching as every possessed looking person lunged at her.

"Tell Jeremiah to find me!" she screamed over and over. It became the armor that she used to try and ward off her own mounting terror.

She put on the speed, racing through the Christians in the Coliseum scene, knowing that they were getting to the end and terrified that she wouldn't be able to catch the man before he escaped.

Finally, the last room. Scenes of the end times and a massive dragon guarding the exit. The man flashed through the door and a figure lunged out from a curtain at Cindy. She screamed as he grabbed her before she realized it was Jeremiah.

"One of the witches!" she screamed, pointing at the exit. He ran with her into the parking lot just in time to see the guy get into a dark blue car and take off.

Jeremiah grabbed her hand and together they jumped the hedge separating the church from the synagogue. Seconds later she was throwing herself into the passenger seat of Jeremiah's car even as he was reversing out of the parking space. She slammed her door as he hit the gas and they went flying toward the exit.

"There!" she screamed, pointing to the blue car racing through the traffic light a block down the street to their left.

"Call Mark!" Jeremiah said as he peeled out.

"My phone's in my purse in the office," she realized frantically.

"Grab mine out of the pocket closest to you," he said, shifting slightly in his seat while keeping his hands glued to the wheel and his eyes on the car ahead of them.

Cindy reached into his pocket and grabbed the phone.

"Jeremiah, what is it?" Mark said as he answered.

"It's Cindy. We've just left the church. We're in the car chasing down one of the witches. It's this creepy looking guy. I can't tell how old he is. He's in a blue car."

"Does he know you're following him?"

"Does he know we're following him?" Cindy parroted.

"No," Jeremiah said. "He thinks he got away clean. I'm tailing him and he'll never see me."

"Did you hear that?" Cindy asked.

"I did. Stay on the line with me and tell me where you're heading so we can jump on him when he gets where he's going. With any luck he'll lead us to the others."

For the next twenty minutes Cindy's heart was in her throat as she strained to keep her eyes on the blue car, losing it more often than not, but trusting in Jeremiah. She told Mark as they made directional changes. At one point he got excited because apparently they'd entered an area where they'd lost a different car they'd been tracking earlier.

"Trina, Liam, and I are probably about a mile behind you," he said.

The suburbs gradually gave way to some smaller patches of farmland that lay between Pine Springs and the forest proper. The farther they went the more distance Jeremiah had to keep between them and the blue car and Cindy became increasingly terrified that they'd lose it altogether.

At last it turned into a farmhouse. Jeremiah slowed up and parked behind a clump of bushes at the side of the road. Then he eased out of the car and looked around.

He got back in. "We're here," he said.

Cindy conveyed the information to Mark.

"Why did he come by the church?" he asked.

"I don't know. He was in line for the maze. I figured out who he was, and here we all are."

"Okay. We'll be there shortly. We got held up by a train that's taking its own sweet time," Mark growled.

Cindy hung up and handed the phone to Jeremiah, relaying the information.

"We've got to get in there," Jeremiah said, his voice low and urgent. "I'm not sure the prisoners have a few minutes to wait, especially not if other members of his coven think there's any chance he was followed."

Cindy had been about to say the same thing. She had that sick feeling in the pit of her stomach again.

They crept silently out of the car and seeing no one outside the farmhouse they ran forward as quietly as possible. Just before the actual house was a barn that was a few feet off the highway. Jeremiah pointed to it and Cindy nodded, having gotten the same feeling that he did.

They managed to make it to the cover of the barn unseen. At least, she thought they did. They crept along behind it until they reached a door. Jeremiah went through first and she followed, closing it behind her. They had been plunged into total darkness. Worse there were a lot of horrible smells in the place, including blood.

Jeremiah took her hand and they crept forward quietly. She would have given anything for a light, but knew they couldn't risk it. Her heart was pounding in her chest and her stomach was twisting harder and harder.

And then, in the darkness, she heard a mewing sound. It was coming from her right. It sounded like a kitten. She wondered if it was one of the stolen cats from the humane society.

They kept walking straight ahead and the mewing got louder. She felt like the kitten was crying out for help and the sound grabbed at her and wouldn't let go. She pulled to the right. After a moment Jeremiah let go of her hand. She felt her way slowly forward. Her eyes were beginning to adjust. There was a shuttered window higher up in the barn that was still letting through slivers of moonlight. Slowly she was able to make things out and she finally saw a cage with a tiny paw reaching out through the bars.

She dropped to her knees and touched the paw.

Suddenly there was a lot more light as the front door of the barn opened. She could see seven people silhouetted in the door, one of them being supported by two of the others. The kitten gave out a high-pitched cry that she was sure could be heard for miles.

"I thought I sedated all those blasted animals. They should have been out by now. Shut that cat up," a woman's voice snapped.

Cindy's fingers fumbled with the door of the cage and she was able to silently open it. She reached in and grabbed the kitten and pulled him out, closing the cage behind him. Then she slipped behind a line of barrels, clutching the tiny ball of fur to her chest. He was purring now and it was shaking his entire body, but at least he wasn't yowling.

She could see through two barrels as a man knelt down next to the cage. He stood up a minute later. "Looks like they're all out cold now," he said, moving back to join the others.

"Then it's time we get this over with."

Cindy had no idea where Jeremiah was, but she prayed that Mark and the others would show up soon.

Six of the people moved to the middle of the barn, forming a loose circle. The seventh walked over to the far side and grabbed something which he then dragged across the floor and deposited on the ring of the circle.

"Lizzie!" the coven member who was injured spat.

"We need her until we perform the last ritual. Then she can be both coven member and sacrifice," the older woman said. "You'll get your chance at her. Lacey, go grab one of the others."

A girl departed the circle and came back a minute later with another girl whose hands and feet were tied but who was still fighting for all she was worth. Cindy's heart flew into her throat and she held the kitten tighter. They weren't planning on sacrificing the girl right there were they?

When they reached the circle one of the men stepped forward and together he and Lacey dropped the other girl onto the ground. Cindy raised up a little higher to see what they were doing and realized they were anchoring her hands and feet to stakes.

Flashbacks to seeing the dead girl in the basement overwhelmed her and bile rose into her mouth. They were planning on killing the girl right then and there. As the two tied her the others began to chant.

And through her terror a word bubbled up from deep inside her and came out. "No!"

Everyone froze, even Cindy.

"What was that?" the old woman asked.

Cindy put the kitten down on the ground behind the barrels, wanting it to be safe. She stood up and strode forward. "I said, 'no'!" she exclaimed defiantly.

She was crazy. She knew that in the back of her mind, but she couldn't stop herself. It was like something else propelled her forward, spoke with such authority through her mouth.

"What did you say?" the old woman cackled.

"In the name of God and Jesus Christ His Son I will not permit you to do this thing," Cindy boomed. She could hear her own voice filling the barn and reverberating around it. And she meant every word. What was happening here was evil and all that it took for evil to flourish was for good men to do nothing. She would not permit it. She would do something.

"Grab her," the witch said.

One of the men lunged forward. Before he could reach Cindy, Jeremiah stepped out of the darkness like her own avenging angel and dropped the man to the ground. She didn't know if he'd killed him and she didn't care. She kept her eyes focused on her other enemies.

The old woman snarled and raised her hand toward Cindy. A tiny, black blur streaked past Cindy and launched itself at the old woman's legs. When the kitten attacked her she suddenly staggered backward a step and fell, hitting her head against one of the support beams. She hit the ground seemingly unconscious. The others stared at their fallen leader for a moment, frightened, then ran for the door.

Mark, Trina, and Liam stepped into the doorway, guns drawn. "Freeze!" Mark shouted. Moments later the coven members were on the ground being handcuffed by Mark and Liam. Trina had gone over to inspect the fallen older woman. When Cindy joined her she glanced up, startled, moving her hands off the woman's head.

"Is she dead?" Cindy asked.

Trina nodded. "That will teach her," she said.

"To what?" Cindy asked, somewhat dazed.

"To mess with the mother of a black cat," Trina said with a small smile.

The kitten was sitting there, staring up at Cindy. She reached down and scooped up the tiny creature and pressed him to her cheek.

"I saw what happened right as we got here. He saved your life. She was getting ready to throw her knife at you," Trina said.

"That's why her hand was raised," Cindy said, feeling slightly dazed.

"Yes," Trina said. "God was looking out for you."

Cindy's hands were shaking and the little kitten was purring again so hard that he was shaking, too. She kissed the top of his head. "God was looking out for both of us," she whispered.

Jeremiah had freed the girl on the ground and she led him to a storage room where the others were being held. In a moment all the kidnap victims were in the middle of the barn having their bonds cut from them. Brenda raced over and hugged Cindy tight.

"This is Meghan, Sarah's sister," Jeremiah said, indicating the girl who the coven had been about to sacrifice.

"Thank you for saving me," she whispered.

"You're welcome, but God was the one in charge, not Me."

Brenda went over and hugged Meghan.

More officers showed up and began taking away the coven members. "I don't understand one thing," Mark finally said when he had a moment. "Why did the one guy show up at the church? I mean, if he hadn't, we never would have found this place. Not in time at any rate."

"I can answer that," Meghan said shakily. They took me into the house to talk to me about my cousin Casey. I think they were afraid of what she might have told the police. Brenda had told everyone that if anyone managed to get to a phone we should call the church because there were people there who could help and that Cindy would make sure that the detective and our rabbi knew what was going on. She made us all memorize the number. While I was in the house I got my chance and I went for it. There was a ton of static and I tried to tell where we were and what was happening. I had no idea how much the woman who answered heard. When they caught me, though, I told them that the people at the church knew everything. As the old lady was taking me back to the barn she called one of the others and told him to check out the church and see who had gotten the call, see if there was any reason to worry. And then you all came," Meghan said, eyes filling with tears.

"I got that call," Cindy said. "And I couldn't hear you, but God did. I know He worked it out so that we could find you because of your bravery."

Meghan shook her head. "I wasn't brave. I was scared. I knew they were going to kill us if we didn't do anything."

"Your call still saved us," Brenda said, hugging her tight.

Lizzie was sitting by herself, having finally come to, and Mark went and put his coat over her shoulders. He gave her his phone and Cindy could hear her calling Traci. There had been a girl and a boy freed that none of the rest of them knew, but they sat huddled with Brenda and Meghan, waiting to be taken home.

Cindy finally found a bale of hay and sat down on it, still clutching the kitten. After a couple of minutes Jeremiah walked over. "It looks like the other cats are going to be fine, just a bit groggy. All the shelter cats are there, plus one that has a collar and a nametag that says Ebony. Lizzie said they were using blood and bits of fur from the cats in the ritual. They also used a lot of other things, most of which I don't even want to know about so I'm certainly not going to share."

"Thank you."

"Anyway, the cats are all scared, but they should be fine once they get back to the shelter."

She shook her head. "No. These cats have already been through enough. They're going to go to good homes even if I have to handpick the families."

Jeremiah nodded and then pointed toward the little cluster of survivors. Brenda and Sarah each were petting a cat.

"I think you've already found homes for two of them, at least."

"Three. Blackie here is mine," she said protectively.

"I don't think anyone will argue that," Jeremiah told her, putting his arm around her. She leaned her head on his shoulder.

"You were amazing," he said softly. "Crazy, but amazing."

"I was just doing what God wanted me to do," she said.

"That still takes a lot of courage," he said, kissing the top of her head. "Just another reason why I love you."

She smiled and felt a warm glow at that. She took a deep breath and allowed herself to relax as she looked around the barn. Everything was going to be okay.

It was amazing how the word had spread like wildfire about everything that had happened. By Friday afternoon all of the black cats from the shelter had found families and Cindy had personally screened each one, stressing the trauma the cats had been through and how heroic they had been.

The haunted house had ended up having four hour lines its opening night and looked to do even better for its last two nights. Word had spread that two of the girls playing monsters inside had nearly been sacrificed by witches and it seemed every kid in a sixty mile radius was willing to go to a church to say they had seen them. Dave had cheerfully found a place in the maze for Meghan near her sister.

The only dark spot was that one of the men from the coven had managed to escape police custody on Tuesday night by faking illness and then knocking out the officers whose car he was riding in. Mark had the entire police force out looking for him, but the whole thing was compounded by the fact that no one knew his name and the only really reliable witness to have gotten a good enough look at him to ever be able to identify him was Lizzie.

Lizzie had been reunited with Traci but there was talk that she'd be going into Federal protective custody pending the outcome of the manhunt that was on for the man. Cindy hoped he was caught soon so all of them could breathe easy and Lizzie could stay at home and continue the healing process.

Five o'clock hit and Cindy turned off her computer. "You going to stick around and see the craziness tonight?" Geanie asked.

"Nope. I've got a date with a kitten. I promised Blackie we'd snuggle on the couch and watch some movies tonight. He's settling in well, but I know he misses me during the day and I'll be gone all tomorrow."

"Give him a scratch behind the ears for me," Geanie said. "When are you introducing him to Jeremiah's dog?"

"We were thinking maybe sometime next week after Blackie's settled in a bit more."

"I'll see you tomorrow morning," Geanie said.

"Wouldn't miss it."

As they exited the office and locked the door Cindy stared in amazement. The line outside the gym was already wrapping three times and the haunted house wasn't even opening for another hour.

"Definitely more people are going to be here than last night," Geanie said.

"Well, Dave got his wish. He's getting all the unchurched kids here one way or another."

And given all the horror she'd seen in the last week, she couldn't think of a better thing than that.

23

Cindy had to admit that Geanie and Joseph knew how to throw a party. The couple had certainly taken the Addam's Family theme to the extreme. They had hired a few local handymen to put up a false facade on the front of their house to make it look like a spooky old mansion and they had redressed everything inside on the bottom floor to fit the theme as well.

She had just walked into the ballroom with the two of them as they were doing final inspections before the party was to begin.

"My darling, how long has it been since we danced?" Joseph asked dramatically, taking Geanie by the hand.

Geanie spun into his arms. "Oh, Joseph. Hours." They giggled as they spun around the room and Cindy couldn't help but smile. The two of them were so well-matched it was ridiculous. Plus she had finally watched the first film the night before and she got the reference.

"It's going to be an awesome party," Cindy said as they came spinning back and stopped next to her.

"More than you can guess," Geanie said with a mysterious smile. If there was one thing Geanie loved, it was surprises and Cindy couldn't even guess what the other woman might have in store for the evening.

"Well, ladies, shall we get ready for the festivities?" Joseph asked with a smile.

Geanie nodded and grabbed Cindy's arm. "I'm just sorry that in having you come early I've robbed you of the chance to arrive at the party in style."

"What do you mean?"

"We're using the parking lot at the bottom of the hill and having people ride up it in a horse drawn carriage," Joseph said. "Maybe if we hurry, though, we'll all have time to ride down and back up with the first guests."

"Yes, perfect! I knew there was a reason I married you," Geanie said flirtatiously. "Now, Cindy and I will get dressed in our room. You can get dressed in your office."

"Banished again! How cruel, how heartless, I like it," Joseph said melodramatically. He was clearly working on getting into character.

Cindy went upstairs with Geanie and once they were in the master bedroom Geanie started giggling like she was losing her mind.

"What is it?"

"I can't tell you, but it's going to be epic," Geanie said.

"Okay, then let's see your dress."

Geanie walked over to a garment bag hanging on a hook on the wall and pulled out a perfect replica of the Morticia dress from the movie.

"Wow," Cindy said as Geanie brought it over. "Is that the real one?"

"No. I made this one."

"You made it?"

"Yup. I made Joseph's costume, too. The hardest part was finding the right materials."

Cindy shook her head in amazement. It was just part of the enigma that was Geanie and Joseph. They had all the money in the world and had bought her an expensive, authentic dress from the actual film she loved, and yet when it came to their costumes Geanie had made them herself instead of tracking down the originals or paying someone else to make them.

She shouldn't have been surprised. Part of the reason she was there early was Geanie had enlisted her help making some of the finger foods for the party even though the desserts were being provided by a caterer.

"You must have put a lot of work into this," she said, admiring the dress.

"It took weeks," Geanie said. "But, it will all be worth it tonight. I'm planning on getting lots of pictures."

"Did you hire a photographer?"

"No, I figured we could just use our cameras. You think I should have?"

"Nah. Everyone will be taking a million pictures with their phones anyway."

"That's what I thought."

Geanie ended up doing Cindy's hair and makeup for her, and she was blown away by the results when she finally saw herself in the mirror. Once she put the dress on and had safety pinned it so it was nice and snug on top she twirled in the dress.

Geanie clapped her hands. "You look like a real Spanish señorita!" She gave her a little curtsey, "Señorita de la Vega!"

"I can't believe it," Cindy said, admiring the entire effect in the full-length mirror in the room.

"Believe it, you look amazing," Geanie said as she set to work on her own hair.

Forty-five minutes later Cindy was seated across from Geanie and Joseph in a black Cinderella style carriage drawn by four massive black horses as it rolled slowly down the hill. It really did feel like they were driving in style and it helped Cindy get into the mood of a character from a bygone era.

They reached the lower parking lot just as a familiar car was pulling up. Mark stepped out of the car. He looked beyond tired. His movements were slow and his face was haggard. Cindy was stunned to see that he was actually wearing a costume. He was dressed up like Dick Tracy.

The passenger side door opened and Lizzie appeared, looking a lot better than the last time Cindy had seen her. Together they walked up to the carriage. Joseph opened the door and the two climbed in settling next to Cindy.

The driver turned the horses and in short order they were heading up the hill back toward the mansion. Mark leaned his head back.

"Trina's heading out of town tonight and is going to take Lizzie with her into protective federal custody until the rest of the coven is caught. Trina had some stuff to take care of this afternoon, though, so we decided to meet here," Mark explained.

"We're happy to help in any way that we can," Joseph said.

"I figured we were probably safer here than at home."

Whatever the reason Cindy was relieved that Mark wouldn't be alone that night. A couple minutes later the driver pulled up in front of the mansion with a grand flourish.

"Wow," Lizzie said as she stepped out of the carriage.

Even Mark managed to look impressed.

"Let's head inside and start attacking the food table," Geanie said cheerily as she disembarked.

That was precisely what the four of them did. Within five minutes other people began to arrive and the energy in the air was high as people laughed and admired the theming for the party.

Half an hour later the orchestra began playing and couples began migrating to the ballroom. Cindy went along to watch and admire some of the dancers who moved with such grace and ease across the floor that she couldn't help but wonder if they were professional dancers. The orchestra seemed to be playing a mixture of Halloween themed tunes and the scores from different films.

As one song was coming to an end a thickly accented Spanish voice spoke behind her. "May I have this dance?"

She turned, getting ready to tell whoever it was that she didn't really dance. She froze before she could say anything, though.

She was staring at Zorro.

He swept low in a courtly bow and when he straightened he gave her a dazzling smile that she recognized.

It was Jeremiah dressed up in a Zorro costume, right down to the cloak and sword. He offered her his hand and she placed hers in it.

"I have to warn you, señor, I'm not a very good dancer," she admitted.

"That is alright. As it turns out, I'm an excellent dancer," he said.

He put his other arm around her waist and a moment later he had swept her onto the dance floor just as the first strains of *I Want to Spend My Lifetime Loving You* began to play. It was the love theme from *The Mask of Zorro*.

Jeremiah was right. He was an amazing dancer and with gentle but firm moves of his hands he guided her in where to go, when to turn, until it felt like they were flying across the floor and that she knew how to dance as well. The more she relaxed into his arms, the more she trusted him, the faster they danced, beginning to move across the floor as one.

Everything else faded away until there was only the two of them and the music driving them onward. When at last it stopped, he twirled her in his arms and then walked with her side-by-side off the dance floor.

"Zorro. Geanie's idea?" she asked, trying to catch her breath.

"Yes, she told me that it would be perfect. Now I see why."

Cindy leaned her head on Jeremiah's shoulder as they walked. Everywhere she looked she saw smiling people in costumes of all sorts. A group of young women had dressed up like the Greek muses and were posing on the grand staircase while a lanky photographer took their picture.

"You look amazing," Jeremiah said.

"You're pretty gorgeous yourself."

They strolled outside, taking in some of the cool, crisp night air. After a few minutes they returned inside and walked into the sitting room where chairs and couches were draped in black fabric. Mark was sitting on one of the couches, phone pressed to his ear.

"It's nearly a perfect night," Cindy commented.

"Nearly?" Jeremiah questioned.

"I wish Traci had come."

"Maybe she'll come around still. At least she knows her sister is safe."

Cindy nodded. She didn't see Lizzie and she wondered if the F.B.I. agent had already come to get her. "I wish they'd caught all the members of the coven. I'm sure once they do, Lizzie will be able to breathe easier."

"All of us will. I'd be willing to bet, though, that whoever they haven't rounded up yet is long gone."

Her eyes drifted around the room and she realized she was looking for Lizzie, but she didn't see her anywhere. Maybe Trina had already come to get her.

Mark got off the phone and they started to walk toward him when Cindy stopped suddenly, a shudder going through her entire body.

"What is it?" Jeremiah asked.

"The photographer taking the picture of the girls on the stairs," Cindy said, realization dawning on her.

"Yeah?"

"He's not supposed to be here. Geanie and Joseph didn't hire a photographer."

"Mark! Where's Lizzie?" Jeremiah asked, moving quickly toward the detective.

Mark frowned and glanced around the room before standing up. "She went to the bathroom a few minutes ago. She should have been back by now."

"I think someone's gotten to her," Cindy said.

"What?"

Jeremiah didn't have time to answer. He was already on his way back to the foyer. The photographer who had been there just a few minutes before was gone. Jeremiah ran outside, Cindy on his heels, where they found the carriage driver unhitching his horses. He had the first one completely freed and was holding it by the bridle it was still wearing.

"Sorry, animals are taking a break until the end of the evening," the man said.

"Did you see a tall man come through here, possibly with a woman?" Jeremiah asked.

"Yeah. Two or three minutes ago. He seemed to be in quite a hurry. Of course, he had a very pretty young woman in his arms, carrying her real romantic."

"Where did they go?"

"They headed for the parking lot."

Jeremiah took three running steps and jumped on top of the horse. With an exclamation the man let go of the bridle as Jeremiah kicked the animal forward.

"It's an emergency!" he heard Cindy shouting at the man.

The horse leaped forward and Jeremiah urged him down the hill. They raced down the path, the wind stinging his eyes. The moon sailed high overhead turning the road into a ribbon of light.

They pounded into the parking lot and Jeremiah saw a man ahead of him carrying a woman who was limp in his arms. Jeremiah raced up close then dismounted in one step as he brought the horse to a halt.

The man spun with an oath, dropped Lizzie on the ground, and then stepped to the side. From his waistband he yanked a wicked looking knife. It was very ornate and he guessed it was a ceremonial dagger that the man had taken to use for more than just rituals.

Jeremiah unsheathed his sword, thankful that Geanie had insisted that he wear a real weapon with his costume. The man lunged forward and Jeremiah easily parried and then stabbed him in the arm. The knife dropped from the man's hands. He warred with himself for a moment. It was always safer to kill your enemies than to let them come back to haunt you another day. Before he could make that decision, though, he heard running footsteps.

"Looks like it was a good thing I was late to the party."

Jeremiah turned and saw Liam standing there, dressed as a gangster complete with Tommy gun. He twisted the other way and saw Mark and Cindy running down the hill toward them. They arrived, breathless, a moment later.

"Evening folks, I'm Al Capone," Liam said with a smirk.

"Is that gun real?" Mark asked, doing a bit of a double take.

"You know it is. Told you my grandfather was a collector."

"You came as a gangster?"

"I always thought a good costume should be the opposite of who you are. Capone was a historical Italian mob boss. I'm a modern Irish cop. Doesn't get much more opposite than that."

"I'm bleeding here!" the man Jeremiah had stabbed said.

"Be grateful you're just bleeding," Mark said darkly as Cindy moved to check on Lizzie.

A car pulled into the parking lot and a minute later Trina got out, dressed like a witch. "Looks like I missed the party," she said.

"Almost. You get to be here for the after party, though, and sometimes those are the best part," Mark said.

Ultimately Trina still took Lizzie with her until they could be sure that they had gotten all the members of the coven, although it looked like with the capture of the last guy they had. Other officers came and carted the man Jeremiah had fought off to jail and Mark, Liam, Cindy and Jeremiah headed back to the party. Jeremiah and Cindy had actually ridden back up the hill on the horse and the way Cindy was looking at Jeremiah made Mark smile. It was the look of a woman in love.

Now that all the excitement was over Mark felt the need to collapse even more strongly. He headed for the ballroom. He wanted to tell Geanie and Joseph that he was heading home and thank them for everything. Inside he skirted the crowd as he looked for them, but he didn't see them. Finally he stood still, debating how bad it would be to just take off and talk to them in a couple of days.

Behind him he heard several people start to wolf whistle. He wondered what woman was the object of so much overt admiration. The whistles grew to such a volume that he finally turned, curious as to what exactly was going on.

There, slinking toward him in the most low cut black dress he had ever seen was Traci. She was swaying her hips in a highly exaggerated way and walking right toward him. She had crimped her hair, put on siren red lipstick, and was wearing pearls. All those he noticed out of the corner of his eyes since he couldn't take his eyes off the dress. Her new curves were there for all the world to see and as the crowd parted around her all the men were casting appreciative looks her way.

She stopped in front of him and before he could even blink she said in a sultry voice, "Hello, Dick. You can call me...Breathless."

"Traci, I-"

She put a finger over his lips and made a shushing sound. "Dick, don't you dare go and spoil my entrance. It seems to me what we need right now is a little more action and a lot less talk."

He grabbed her hard and kissed her, molding her body to his. He could hear a few catcalls and whistles, but he just kept kissing her. When he finally let go both of them were breathless.

"Get a room!" he heard someone say humorously.

"I intend to," Mark said. He grabbed her hand and pulled her through the crowd. They made it out of the ballroom and headed for the staircase.

"Dick, where are we going?" she asked, still using her vixen voice.

He turned to her and let his eyes sweep her body. "Morticia and Gomez have five thousand bedrooms in this house and we're going to find one that's vacant."

"And then?" she asked, her breath catching a little bit.

He leaned in close and brushed his lips against her ear. "I hope you didn't pay too much for the dress because I'm going to rip it off of you."

He swept her up into his arms and carried her up the stairs, kissing her every step of the way.

.

I WILL FEAR NO EVIL

260

Look for

THOU ART WITH ME

The next book in the Psalm 23 Mysteries series

Coming February 2015

Look for

THE BROTHERHOOD OF LIES

Book 2 in the Tex Ranvencroft Adventures

Coming Winter 2015

Look for

THE SUMMER OF RICE CANDY

Book 5 in the Sweet Seasons series

Coming Winter 2015

Debbie Viguié is the New York Times Bestselling author of more than three dozen novels including the *Wicked* series, the *Crusade* series and the *Wolf Springs Chronicles* series co-authored with Nancy Holder. Debbie also writes thrillers including *The Psalm 23 Mysteries,* the *Kiss* trilogy, and the *Witch Hunt* trilogy. When Debbie isn't busy writing she enjoys spending time with her husband, Scott, visiting theme parks. They live in Florida with their cat, Schrödinger.

Printed in Great Britain
by Amazon.co.uk, Ltd.,
Marston Gate.